PRIMARY BENEFICIARY

DAVID L. TACKETT

Strategic Book Publishing and Rights Co.

Copyright © 2017 David L. Tackett. All rights reserved.

No part of this book may be reproduced or transmitted in any form or by any means, graphic, electronic, or mechanical, including photocopying, recording, taping, or by any information storage retrieval system, without the permission, in writing, of the publisher. For more information, send an email to support@sbpra.net, Attention: Subsidiary Rights.

Strategic Book Publishing and Rights Co., LLC
USA | Singapore
www.sbpra.com

For information about special discounts for bulk purchases, please contact Strategic Book Publishing and Rights Co., LLC, Special Sales, at bookorder@sbpra.net.

ISBN: 978-1-68181-442-1

ACKNOWLEDGEMENTS

One morning while in a San Antonio, Texas, hotel room overlooking the Riverwalk, my wife Patty awakened and looked to see what I was doing. I was sitting in a chair holding a pen and the small scratch pad that usually sits beside the phone in a typical hotel room.

"What are you doing?"

I replied, "I'm writing a novel."

Several years later when I typed the words "The end," a feeling of accomplishment swept over me like I had never felt before.

I would never have been able to complete this book without the encouragement of my wife Patty and our children Bryan, Chris and Courtney. They have always supported me. I love them for the trust they have in me as their husband and father. I'm proud of my family.

Fran Rephan…she was the first to type then re-type and correct my mistakes while encouraging me to continue.

Joyce Stacks…editor

Chris Carson…my guardian angel.

If you are from Atkins or Hot Springs, Arkansas, or Lawrence, Kansas, you may recognize the names of some of my friends. I found it easier to write if I could put a name and face with my characters.

I had fun making them be people opposite from their true selves. I hope everyone enjoys reading their names. This is a book of fiction.

TABLE OF CONTENTS

CHAPTER 1 - PROVIDERS 7
CHAPTER 2 - EVERYONE STARTS SOMEWHERE 10
CHAPTER 3 - CHUCK BEFORE FREEWAY 16
CHAPTER 4 - A MATCH TO LIGHT THE FIRE 24
CHAPTER 5 - LOST AND NOT FOUND 32
CHAPTER 6 - THE METER IS RUNNING: FAST 34
CHAPTER 7 - BRINGING IT TOGETHER STRAIGHT AND NARROW 37
CHAPTER 8 - "IN FORCE" 40
CHAPTER 9 - FRATERNIZING 48
CHAPTER 10 - SOUNDS OF SILENCE 50
CHAPTER 11 - CUT AND DRIED 52
CHAPTER 12 - TRIFECTA 55
CHAPTER 13 - LYING AND TRYING 57
CHAPTER 14 - SOMETIMES, MOE WASN'T ALWAYS LUCKY 59
CHAPTER 15 - THE GOOD OL' DAYS 60
CHAPTER 16 - SIGHT FOR SORE EYES 65
CHAPTER 17 - BURN A LITTLE LESS HOT 69
CHAPTER 18 - A PROMISE IS A PROMISE 72
CHAPTER 19 - NO EVIDENCE 76
CHAPTER 20 - WORKING TOGETHER HARMONIOUSLY 78
CHAPTER 21 - SLEIGHT OF HAND 84
CHAPTER 22 - SERVED WITH A SIDE OF NATIVE 89
CHAPTER 23 - DADDY'S KNOW 90
CHAPTER 24 - BEHIND THE STABLE DOOR 93

CHAPTER 25 - SIGNED, SEALED, DELIVERED 95
CHAPTER 26 - AN ASSET 99

CHAPTER 1
PROVIDERS

Bradley and Tony had been friends throughout high school. However, acquaintances might be a better word for their relationship, as friends would be stretching it.

Bradley was fierce and widely considered a leader and competitor both on and off of the football field. As tailback for the Lakeside High School Stampede, he led the school to state playoffs for three consecutive years. Before that, it had been twelve years since the team had been to the playoffs, that is until Bradley Clevenger, a sixteen-year-old sophomore was named starting tailback. He seemingly had that next gear to shift into whenever he broke through the line of scrimmage, and with daylight between him and the goal line, he was seldom tackled from behind.

There's something about having a winning team to support and follow that brings together fans from every walk of life. In fact, on Friday nights when the Stampede played on their home field, most of the town's 40,000 residents could be found either watching from inside the stadium or in the parking lot drinking beer and listening to Dick Antione doing the play-by-play on KZNG 1340AM.

In the eyes of the locals, Bradley could do no wrong. As long as he was scoring touchdowns and the Stampede kept winning, Bradley Clevenger appeared to have life's blessings in the palm of his hands. The banker in town was always standing at the edge of the goal line to shake Bradley's hand as he walked off of the field. After a while, it became customary for Bradley to start looking for him as soon as the final buzzer signaled that the game was over.

However, what set this banker apart from any other appreciative fan was the fact that immediately following the congratulatory hand shake and pat on the back, Bradley would discover a hundred dollar bill for every touchdown he had scored that night neatly deposited in his hand.

In terms of his school work, Bradley studied just hard enough to collect a *B* average in order to make the school's *Stampede List*, this being a list of all of the students who had scored a 3.0 GPA or better. These students were not required to take their finals unless they were trying to raise their grade; however, Bradley never tried to raise his grade. He was quite satisfied with a B average. Had he have taken a book home to study for an exam, he could've certainly pulled off an *A*, especially if the subject had been math. Bradley was always very good with numbers.

Built from the same template as Michelangelo's *David*, Bradley's calf muscles appeared to have had grapefruit implants. His thighs were chiseled same as if they were tree trunks, and if truth be known, his rear end attracted glances from both sexes. Few girls in the Stampede's senior class had a smaller waistline than Bradley's, while the construction workers' shoulder-length, summer-blond hair topping off his 6'2" frame made him easy to spot in a crowd. Most of his female classmates – not to mention several of the school's youngest teachers – would have broken both hearts and rules to have had a few stolen moments alone with the star of the Lakeside High Stampede.

One might say Bradley had it all: good looks fit for a *Gentlemen's Quarterly* cover spread, physique, charisma, good grades, and the kind of drive necessary to be somebody. Bradley had wanted to be his own boss from the beginning, independent and running his own business. He was always saying things like, "A high percentage of the American working population can be classified as professional clock punchers. They want to be told what time to go to work, what time to get off, even what to eat during their 15 minute break, according to the vending machines that offer either Twinkies or Hostess Cup Cakes. The most difficult decision clock punchers make all week is what kind of beer they're going to drink on the weekend. Only 10 to 20 percent of the working American population actually owns the time clocks inside their own businesses, and it's the time clock owners who make most of the big money. They live big, vacation big, and drive big, while the clock punchers make just enough money throughout the course of an entire year to either take a two week vacation or stay home and paint their houses." But they can't afford to do both.

Yes, Bradley wanted to be a time clock owner. He wanted to

own a house in East Gate Subdivision, the gated community where most of the upper income homeowners resided, or at least lived there while pretending to be upper income.

Tony LaTour had been one of Bradley's friends (OK, acquaintance). He also had a drive to be successful; however, making an *A* on his report card had never been a top priority. He looked upon the students with perfect grades as either nerds or momma's boys who studied every Saturday night. Tony's stomach turned sour whenever he thought about *those* types of students. In his mind, straight *A's* meant they'd run home from school brandishing their report cards in order to get a hug from their mommies, maybe some cookies and milk while listening to their mothers softly coo, "Honey, with all *A's* you'll probably become a doctor or lawyer, and be able to take care of your mother in her old age."

No, Tony didn't want to become a doctor or lawyer. He didn't want to be on call most days and every third weekend. The LaTour family had once lived next door to a doctor, and Tony had seen that same doctor rushing off to the hospital at all hours of the day and night. He thought back to a Super Bowl Sunday and remembered seeing the doctor speed off toward the hospital during the first quarter of the game and thought, "I'd let that inconsiderate bastard die if he couldn't find a better time to get sick than during the Super Bowl."

Tony often thought of doctors as legal dealers or *providers*. At least they could certainly provide for their patients. They could write out prescriptions all day long for drugs that would enable one to party all night. While Tony also possessed the desire for a lot of money, there was one major difference that set Bradley and him apart: he was going to be a provider, but not in a profession that required eight years of college. No, he had already been educated on the streets as a provider of alcohol, drugs, hookers, and gambling. As long as there was Friday nights, both Bradley and Tony were destined to be providers. Bradley provided the thrills during the ballgame, and Tony would provide the thrills afterward.

CHAPTER 2
EVERYONE STARTS SOMEWHERE

Tony had struggled in school. It was a cause for celebration whenever he pulled down a report card with all *C's*. In fact, most semesters Tony picked out a couple of different girls to help him with his grades. First, he'd play up to some plain Jane wrapper who typed with both speed and accuracy. Then, he would turn on the charm, knowing his year-end reports would be typed perfectly. For math class, he usually found a campus beauty with a fondness for diet pills, and essentially the deal was made. Tony would keep her speeding while she completed Tony's homework assignments. However, the only math that really interested Tony was counting his money at the end of each day.

He lived by the law of the jungle: only the strongest, fastest, and most cunning animals survived. In Africa, when the sun comes up, the gazelle knows that it has to run faster than the fastest lion, or that day will be his last. Conversely, every lion knows it must run faster than the slowest gazelle, or on that day the lion goes hungry. In the end, regardless of whether you're a lion or a gazelle, when the sun comes up in Africa, you'd better start running. In America, the same is true, but asphalt covers the jungle while humans go in search of their prey.

As a freshman in high school, Tony began earning his spending money by way of the LaTour family's interest in race horses. Johnny LaTour was head of the family in Hot Springs and Garland County. As such he ran the local book-making joint. Business was always good. Even when the economy was bad it seemed like gambling was still stronger than ever. Oaklawn Park had been in business for over 100 years and was still considered the premier horse track in America. The live racing season still stretches from January through April, but simulcast goes on year-round. The *Arkansas Derby* caps the last day of live season with the winner automatically qualifying for the Kentucky Derby. As a result, business was always good.

Growing up in a gambling family, Tony instantly learned how to book races. Although being a bookie may be illegal, it was also oh so profitable. During the live season, Tony kept a notebook where he'd write down the bets he booked while still in school. There always seemed to be those students who were willing to risk their lunch money trying to hit the long shot that would turn ten dollars into a hundred or more.

Tony's rules were simple: if you place a bet and your horse finishes in the money, which means in one of the first three spots, then the bettor would receive the payoff minus a 15% handling fee that Tony kept. So, if ten dollars was bet, and the winnings were twenty, then he would pay the bettor seventeen and keep three for himself. However, if that same ten dollars was bet and the horse lost, the ten dollars was all Tony's. Often Tony made a couple thousand dollars per month from his high school booking business alone.

Tony knew something about the horses that the average bettor didn't know, with that being the average bettor thinks either the best horse will win or that the race is fixed before it's even ran. Neither, of course is true. The horse races aren't fixed, but the best horse doesn't always run to win. In most races of eight to ten horses, only 3 or 4 are even trying to win. The others have their sights on a bigger race in the future.

When a trainer realizes that they have a special colt, they start planning well ahead for the day when that horse will be running in the Arkansas Derby, or possibly even the Kentucky Derby. The trainer then visits with the owner and together they begin making plans or strategies for the horse. They want to insure high odds on their own horse when it's entered into the big race. Thus, the trainer enters the colt in a number of smaller races, so the colt becomes experienced at coming out of the gate with other horses and accustomed to hearing the starting bell ring, the metal clanging as the gates fly open. The trainer actually wants the colt to stay in the pack finishing either 4th or 5th. Therefore, the jockey takes no chances and doesn't use the whip.

Only the owner, trainer, and jockey know whether or not they are entered in a race that they actually want to win. In the meantime, they want the colt to gain experience and they want the betting public to lose confidence and money on the colt so that the next time it runs the odds will he higher and the payoff larger.

When they get to the race they want to win, they change their routine. The trainer loads the horse up on vitamins and non-detectable stimulants several hours before the race. He handles the colt differently. The trainer talks with more power and discipline to work the colt into a nervous frenzy. When the jockey mounts, the colt knows immediately that today is different. Today is the day the whip comes out. Today is the day that both take chances. Today is the day to WIN!

The owner has waited years for this day to bet a bundle of money right on the horse's nose to win. The owner, trainer, and jockey bet heavily. If everyone has done their job correctly, the jockey will ride the colt across the finish line as leader of the pack. After all, up to this point their colt has neither run at full speed in a race, nor has the colt ever felt the sting of a whip.

So, when Tony got wind of who was running to win, he would load up on a *place* ticket (which means finishing second) or a *show* ticket (coming in third), and walk away with a full pocket. Tony was smart enough not to get too greedy. Remember, two horses may be running to win. Losing all of your money by a nose, which is determined by a photo finish, can ruin your day. As a rule, Tony usually had a lot of tickets in play on any given day so he was happy winning less money per individual ticket.

Despite the fact the racing season was only about three months long, the trappings were good. He and the LaTour family made plenty of money booking bets during the live race meet, well enough to live in Eastgate with most of the doctors, lawyers, and business owners in Hot Springs.

After the horses left town and Oaklawn Park closed for the season, the clientele of the LaTour's booking business still needed their weekly fix of excitement. So it was basketball and March Madness in the spring, followed by baseball in the summer and football in the fall.

Thus the family did quite well in the small city of Hot Springs, Arkansas.

The town is a unique. Hot water bubbles out of the side of a mountain at approximately 143 degrees overlooking Central Avenue in the heart of the city. Historically, Indians knew this spot as The Valley of Vapors and considered the area to be tribal healing grounds. After a battle between neighboring tribes, the wounded would go to the hot springs to soak and heal their wounds. Therefore it was considered a sacred place where weapons were not allowed. Thus all Native Americans bathed together regardless of tribal affiliation, as no fighting could take place on the holy land lest the spirits of the water turn against its violators.

Eventually, the Indian tribes that used the healing waters were replaced by tribes of a different sort, namely those active in illegal business from all parts of America during the 1920s. Therefore, Hot Springs became widely known for its association with the underworld. Beer and whisky ran freely; even during a time when the rest of the nation found itself encumbered by the law of Prohibition. Casinos lined one side of Central with blackjack tables and slot machines on their 1st floor with the second floor usually reserved for a brothel, while luxurious bath houses lined the opposite side of Central Avenue where the water, known for its therapeutic healing powers, began attracting customers in droves from the world over who all soaked while simultaneously praying for some miraculous cure from dreaded diseases such as polio, tuberculosis and syphilis.

Coincidentally, the Mafia families who ran organized crime used the same unwritten code as their predecessors, the Indians: no weapons were allowed in Hot Springs and there was no fighting between different family factions. Everyone respected this rule. Thus it was not uncommon for several members of different families to be seen in the same restaurant or casino at the same time.

Between the 1920's and the early part of the 1960s, Hot Springs had the finest entertainment found in America. Tony Bennett first sang *I left My Heart in San Francisco* at a club appropriately named The Vapors, situated at the north end of Central Avenue. However, the party came to an end in the spring of 1964 when the newly elected governor of Arkansas, Winthrop Rockefeller, decided to *clean up* Hot Springs. The resulting backlash included closing down whore houses, casinos and finally ridding the city's connection to organized crime. Governor Rockefeller came to office intent on keeping his campaign promises, thus changing the complexion of Hot Springs forever.

But the Mafia didn't just quietly leave town. They simply took their illegal activities to the back alleys or behind so-called legal store fronts such as floral shops, laundromats, and otherwise legitimate businesses.

As a result, the LaTour Family became associated with the Capone Family back in the 1920s. Al Capone spent as much time as was possible in Hot Springs as a permanent resident of the fourth floor of the Arlington Hotel. To this day you can book a room at the Arlington Hotel and stay in the Al Capone Suite. Appropriately, his personal suite faced downtown's Central Avenue. Peering from the balcony, he could see directly into his casino, otherwise known as the Southern Club. Capone made millions from the business conducted there. On any given Saturday night, hundreds of customers took in the strip show, touted as having the best strippers this side of Hollywood, or treated themselves to a night of drinking and gambling. Either way, the money flowed as freely as the whiskey.

Capone also made money by selectively recruiting locals to assist in the gambling ring. Coincidentally, he was introduced to Tony's grandfather, Francis LaTour, following Sunday mass at Saint John the Baptist Catholic Church still situated on West Grand Avenue. That day Francis LaTour simply walked up to Capone in the parking lot and said, "We both have roots that go back to the Motherland, across the waters, beyond the rules and regulations of the native Indians and the current white men. You need me in your organization, and I need to support my heritage."

Francis had dropped out of school during the eighth grade, and later, in his early twenties, found himself to be poor. Capone promised LaTour that loyalty would grant him a position in the Capone Family forever, and that disloyalty would result in the loss of his tongue.

Almost overnight, Capone set up the LaTour Family in the laundry business with Francis' own mother working behind the front counter. She ran the store up front while the phone in the back room rang constantly with people making bets on daily races. Thus, the family's illegitimate business began to flourish. Needless to say the LaTour *Same Day Service Laundry* laundered far more bags of money than it ever did clothes.

Soon, the fabric of the LaTour family began to change in rather obvious ways. It didn't take long before they started driving expensive cars, dressing in fine suits, and dining at equally expensive restaurants. Residents of Hot Springs instinctively knew that the LaTour family had hit pay dirt…from somewhere.

CHAPTER 3
CHUCK BEFORE FREEWAY

Tony learned at a young age how to turn a small amount of money into a larger amount. He loaned money to his classmates and the interest rate he charged was based on how desperately the classmate wanted the loan. They never seemed to have enough money and the price for getting high didn't come cheap. Therefore, since Tony was both the banker and drug pusher, inflation hit hard on both ends of the purchase. High interest on the money and a high mark-up on the product purchased.

He could charge a high rate of interest since the loan was paying for illegal activities, and he was assuming part of the risk. The local bank's single-figure rate of return didn't interest Tony at all, because he saw himself on the fast path to making big money and living large.

He was the person to know if you needed something or, better said, needed *anything*. Students were always going to Tony to take care of their weekend needs – whether that be beer, smokes or recreational drugs. The price was always the same: double the cost. It was worth the money to his clients not to have the hassle of getting caught stealing from their parents, or even worse, not getting their fix at all.

On one Friday afternoon in the early 1970s, students hung out in the parking lot of the Shell gas station on Malvern Avenue. At around 4:00pm, Tony took orders from his classmates for their weekend drink of choice – the final tally usually several hundred dollars' worth of liquor, cigarettes, a few cigars, and an assortment of drugs such as pot, cocaine, and cross-top diet pills used as 'speed'.

As a minor, he needed an accomplice to help him carry out his retail business. Chuck Sorrels was his man. Tony referred to him as *Freeway* and introduced him as his personal chauffeur and bodyguard, even though Freeway actually drove a city cab. Precisely at 4:20pm on Friday afternoon, Freeway would pull into the Shell parking lot, and Tony would jump into the back seat of the black-and-white city cab.

They would go to Freeway's apartment and change cars before going to Finish Line Liquor Store where they would purchase several cases of beer, pints of whiskey, wine, and the occasional bottle of cheap champagne for the stud who thought it was a fitting way to celebrate the night's activities.

After leaving the liquor store, they had to make their drug connection in the alleyway behind the National Park Hotel on Gorge Street – which was a dangerous part of town for two white guys – a strange pair at that with Tony being a baby-faced kid of sixteen, an early thirties hustler sporting a ponytail to the middle of his back and an untrimmed beard while Freeway was still thinking and living in the late 60's. His always present aviator glasses could never hide the fact that his nights were used for partying as opposed to sleeping.

Freeway's cocaine habit couldn't be satisfied with wages he made driving a cab, so Tony and Freeway needed each other equally. Tony's job involved getting the orders for liquor, drugs, and cigarettes, while Freeway had to make the purchases in the liquor store or the alley. Together, they could each make several hundred dollars per week. Tony usually loaned his portion of the profit to Freeway at the non-published rate of fifty percent interest, payable at the beginning of the month. Somehow Freeway always had the money on the first. Tony never asked how – nor did he care to know where the money came from. After all, getting a fifty-percent ROI was higher than any Wall Street deal.

Freeway, a Vietnam veteran, had always been a loser. He had graduated from Hot Springs High School, but he didn't have a clue as to what he wanted to do with his life. In fact, he *assumed* he would be drafted into the military. With his draft number being 175, the army recruiter had told Freeway that he would be receiving his *Greetings* letter from Uncle Sam during the first ten days of August. That was how the military draft worked back then: a nationally televised draft day with ping pong balls painted with the number of each day of the year, all popping about like movie house popcorn in a lottery type bingo machine. If the first ball had the date of February

12th, then everyone with the birthday of February 12th would have a draft day of number 1. If the 100th slot was filled with August 1st, then everyone with that birthday would keep the draft number 100 for the year.

The military could always predict with a degree of certainty what number or how high in the draft lottery they were going to draft during any given year. Constantly keeping this in the back of his mind, Freeway tried to squeeze in as much partying as possible before the army came looking for him sometime during the first half of August.

To make certain his early August draft prediction didn't catch him by surprise, Chuck Sorrels visited the local Armed Services Recruiting Center every Tuesday, the day after the most recent draft notices were mailed. As soon as he entered the recruiting center lined with all branches of the military Chuck would ask, "What number are you on?"

The Army Sergeant always answered. Since ninety percent of all draftees ended up in the army, Sergeant Johnson's desk was the first in a row of four in a shotgun-styled office. Anyone entering the front door of the recruiting office immediately noticed the posters on the wall illustrating exotic places with palm trees and powdered sugar beaches or mountains and waterfalls. A couple of posters of camouflaged soldiers coming out of a swamp hung with the caption reading, "Real Men Do What It Takes". Amongst the cypress trees dripping with hanging moss, it took a few minutes to actually see the Navy Seals.

Sergeant Johnson, just a kid himself of maybe twenty-three or twenty four, loved the military. If he hadn't decided to become a soldier, he could have been a great car salesman. His favorite saying was, "Have I got a deal for you!"

During each weekly visit to the center Chuck asked, "When do you think you will get to number one seventy five?" Sergeant Johnson always replied, "Probably around the middle of August, but if you're in a hurry, I'll see what kind of deal I can get for you."

"Not yet, but I'll talk to you next week," was always Chuck's reply as the door slammed shut behind him.

For several months, Chuck spent most of the summer sleeping until noon, but on rainy days he might stay in bed until midafternoon. Regardless of when he woke up, coffee was his drink of choice for the first hour after rolling out of bed. Next on the agenda: three or four hours of lying on the couch, followed by several phone calls about evening plans. Most nights, the gathering place was Carpenter Dam.

Chuck and several other teenagers would meet at Carpenter Dam State Park, where a man-made dam separated Lake Hamilton and Lake Catherine. With the coals from the previous night's campfire still smoldering, the first person to arrive would get the fire started again. Most of the boys with trucks brought firewood from their homes, or wooden pallets from construction sites, either way; they always had fuel for their gatherings. They preferred pallets because they didn't give off a campfire smell, which was good for the girls who told their parents they were going to the movies. In the middle of summer, the campfire wasn't needed for warmth anymore. Its main purpose was a gathering place. It protected them from getting arrested by the local police on patrol. Since someone usually spotted the patrolman at least several blocks away, the partying crowd would simply toss their joints into the fire, thus burning up the evidence before the police had an opportunity to close in on them.

During that summer of 1970, marijuana was as easy to get as beer. Several of the local farmers grew pot alongside their soybeans and corn. As a cash crop, proceeds from pot made for a much easier income than a normal 8 to 5 job. The farming soil around Hot Springs had the perfect composition for growing pot, slightly sandy with good drainage. Plants would get to the 6 ft. harvest height by the end of the growing season.

Many of those same farmers allowed Chuck to plant pot along the back side of their fields for a small cash donation. Chuck grew the plants, harvested and cleaned his crop, and then sold it in sandwich zip lock bags for twenty dollars an ounce. Chuck, himself, was actually his own best customer, selling what was left to his friends. He was clever in that he wasn't one to take chances by dealing with anyone who wasn't from his childhood. He may not have been afraid of being drafted into the military, but prison was never going to be an address for Chuck Sorrels.

Nightly visits to Carpenter Dam usually started with smoking some home-grown pot, drinking beer or wine, and waiting for the girls to arrive. The girls knew the tradeoff: free beer and pot for thirty minutes or so in the back of a pickup truck, with a Rebel flag as the cover up. The Crosby, Stills, and Nash song *Love the One You're With* described the situation perfectly.

Everyone got what they wanted. Most of the teenagers said this was the summer they would never forget, also a summer they would never be able to discuss with their grandchildren.

When the fire died down around two o'clock in the morning, the party would come to a close. With eight or ten hours of sleep, this same routine was more or less repeated all summer long, until Tuesday, the eighth of August. That's when the weekly visits to the recruiting center came to a screeching halt.

"Hey, Sergeant Johnson, when are you going to call up number 175?"

"Well kid, it looks like you've dodged a bullet," Sergeant Johnson replied. "We've received word that 170 is the last number to be drafted this year." The Sergeant leaned forward in his chair, nodded his head up and down, while looking at Chuck dead center and said, "You must be living right kid."

Chuck had just heard the words that would have made most eighteen year olds ecstatic: not going to be drafted, not going to Vietnam, and not going to be the first soldier from the block that came home in a box. However, he saw it differently. He was not going to *see the world* or *be all you can be*. He was going to be another local loser that just couldn't figure how life worked.

Suddenly, it appeared to Chuck all he was ever going to be was broke, with no job and nothing to do.

"Sergeant Johnson, I should be happy, but I've kept it in the back of my mind that one day I would get my papers and be in the Army for the next three years," Chuck said sadly, as he looked around the room.

The Sergeant asked, "What kind of deal are you looking for son?"

"Two years and a guarantee *not* to go to Vietnam will get my signature."

"I can't do it Chuck," the Army guy said, "The war is going strong and almost everyone goes in-country for at least a year," thinking out loud while rubbing his temples. "Maybe I could get you a deal as a jeep driver."

Chuck didn't respond. Instead he shifted his stare down the hall to the next cubicle where the Navy recruiter was working, "Hey, Swabbie, I'm looking for two years and a guarantee not to go to Vietnam."

"We have a four-year minimum, but with the Navy you will see places you've only dreamed about."

The Navy recruiter started putting pamphlets and brochures together to swing into a presentation about the Navy when Chuck raised his hand in a stop gesture and said, "Sorry, I'm simply not interested."

The Air Force officer gave Chuck the once-over while he stood there with his shoulder length hair parted down the middle, bell-bottomed jeans with a fractured hem dragging the floor, and untucked shirt tail. He resembled a poster to help the homeless rather than that of a leader destined to help save our country.

Chuck turned to look at the Air Force recruiter. The airman snapped his hand out in front of him resembling the same way Diana Ross did while singing *Stop In The name Of Love*. "Whoa Cowboy, don't even think about standing in front of my desk. My Air Force isn't interested in any long-haired, sun-starved idiot whose only goal at this time is to shoot his wad in someone new each week!"

Chuck's hair immediately stood at attention on the back of his neck. He looked at the Air Force nerd and thought, "That skinny son-of-a-bitch had better watch his mouth. Look at him, four-eyed in a pussy-looking uniform. I should slap him into next week."

Their eyes locked for several seconds and then Chuck grinned and said, "You seem to have sized me up quite accurately, and I've decided the feelings are mutual. I don't want any part of you or who you represent, so let's not waste each other's time." Chuck spun around on his heels and headed for the door when he heard a booming voice cut the air from behind him.

"Not so fast marine."

Chuck stopped and peered into the far corner of the office. He didn't remember the Marine Sergeant, a recruiter, or his desk from any of his previous visits. Maybe he had just moved into the office, or maybe he was usually out to lunch when Chuck stopped by, but either way the Marine Sergeant was certainly present now. Chuck walked cautiously toward the desk, obscured by a cloud of cigar smoke hanging in the area. The Sergeant propped his spit-shined shoes upon the desk, where a pearl-handled .45 caliber pistol lay beside a jeweled sword.

The barrel-chested Sergeant started talking, "Son, this Vietnam conflict that's been going on for as long as I can remember is just about to come to an end. Sit down. I've got a few things to tell you." Close to Chuck's ear, in a voice low enough so that no one else could hear he asked, "Oh by the way, do you like Coke with your whiskey or just straight on the rocks?"

Chuck looked into his eyes and saw the soul of someone he immediately liked, with the physique of someone you wanted in your corner if you ended up in a street fight. "I usually drink it with Coke," Chuck said, as he relaxed in the ten-dollar folding chair from Wal-Mart.

"I'll be right back," the Sergeant said, as he went through the door to a kitchen area in the back of the office.

Chuck pulled out a cigarette and lit it then looked around the Sergeant's desk. In a frame on one side of his desk rested a Purple Heart, which meant he had been wounded in the line of duty. The only other picture was one with him hugging Ann Margaret with Bob Hope in the background, obviously taken during one of Hope's ISO Christmas shows in Vietnam. Chuck liked what he saw both on and around the Marine's desk notably, *The Few, The Proud, The Marines* emblazoned into a desktop sign.

The Sergeant came back through the door with two dark-colored glasses, handing one to Chuck. The Sergeant's drink was a fifteen-year-old single malt scotch, neat. "Tell me son, have you ever been with a Filipino woman?" knowing full well that a high school kid from Hot Springs, Arkansas had probably never even seen a woman from the Orient, much less had sex with one. "Well, let me tell you. There's nothing like a young woman from the Philippines. Except for the hair on their head and about a silver dollars' worth of hair on their pussy, those Filipino women have no hair on their bodies at all. If you get in a knot with one of them on a hot summer night, they get so slippery that it's hard to keep them from squirting right out of bed. From my personal experience, there's not a woman in the world that can compare with a woman from the Philippines. They're the best, and lucky for you most of the new recruits joining the Marines today are sent straight to the Philippines. You can sow your wild oats right into the bellies of the most beautiful women in the world."

"Sarge, I don't want to go to Vietnam." Chuck said, looking at him eye-to-eye.

Sarge leaned forward and spoke in a low voice, "Son, I don't believe I've said a damn thing about going to Viet-fucking-Nam. I believe I said that the lucky Maries go to the Philippines. Now let me tell you what happens to the unlucky ones. They stay in sunny California with those same girls the Beach Boys sing about. You know the *I wish they all could be California girls*? Those guys have never been to the Philippines."

"I don't want to be in more than two years," said Chuck, while still eye-to-eye with him.

"That's one of the best things about our program. Some only spend about eighteen months of active duty if they enroll in college and register for classes immediately after returning to the states," Sarge stated, raising his left eyebrow ever so slightly. Staring into each other's souls, the Sergeant slowly leaned back in his chair, never losing eye contact with Chuck. With his teeth clinched together, Chuck's focus drifted to the poster on the wall ... *The Few, The Proud, The Marines*.

It sounded like a shotgun blast when Chuck slammed his hand down on top of the Sergeant's desk, jumping to his feet and shouting, "LET'S DO IT!" he then glanced over his shoulder to give his best *fuck you* look to the Air Force recruiter.

A week later, Chuck was in the Marine Corps boot camp in Parris Island, wondering what in the hell had happened. Twelve weeks later, Chuck was riding in the belly of a huge troop carrier headed to Vietnam. Three years later after spending a year in the brigade for having a duffel bag full of pot, Chuck received a Dishonorable Discharge from the United Stated Marine Corps. He knew he would never get a good job or make a decent living with that Dishonorable Discharge always hanging over him, but at least he was out of the Marine Corps.

CHAPTER 4
A MATCH TO LIGHT THE FIRE

A few years after graduating from high school, Tony met Jim Boy at the gazebo located in the infield at Oaklawn Park. The infield is an area where spectators can stand in the open air next to the finish line. There they watched the horses come galloping past, slinging mud, blood and beer in all directions. There were also bleachers where one might sit while studying the Racing Form in an attempt to pick out the winner of the upcoming race while mentally counting their chickens before they hatched.

Tony sat on those same concrete bleachers waiting for the fifth race to start. It was a fifty-thousand dollar purse for Arkansas-bred horses. The favorite in the race was named Water Slide, a four year old grey gelding, who was born on Raymond Baker's farm just north of Hot Springs. Water Slide had already won a slew of races, as well as, the following of local fans.

Tony's bookmaking had grown exponentially since his high school days. He now had a mobile home in the northeast part of town near Magic Springs Amusement Park, where he conducted his business. He had removed the beds and replaced them with small desks and lawn chairs. Each bedroom had three phones that rang constantly on race days. There were also radios in the main room tuned in to 1340 AM blaring race results. Scattered around the rooms were copies of the Daily Racing Form for the bettors who stopped by for a free beer or two while deciding on which horse to take a chance.

Several of his wannabe's answered the phones writing down bets in a spiral-bound notebook. Typically thousands of bettors called during the racing season. In Arkansas, betting was illegal outside of Oaklawn Park, so if someone wanted to place a bet without going to the track, he (or she) called Tony. If that horse won, the bettor knew that a 15% handling fee would automatically be deducted from the winnings. That was the one thing that hadn't increased over time since high school.

Occasionally, a big bettor might start zeroing in on a particular horse, and if Tony had heard through the grapevine that the owners were running their horse to win that day, he'd go to the track and bet the bank on that same horse. Then if he happened to win, Tony would have made enough money to pay off the person who had placed the original bet. Then he'd still walk away with a day's worth of money, which was above and beyond his 15% take.

Sitting in the stands at the track, Tony looked up at the clouds. He could see dogs and dinosaurs in the clouds while he contemplated the future. "Two more months and I'm going on a seven day cruise to anywhere," he thought to himself. For a solitary moment he couldn't hear the crowd. Steel drums and reggae music drifted through the park like a rubber raft floating down a gentle stream. Tony heard Terry Wallace, the track announcer, say something about it never raining at Oaklawn Park. That's when he noticed that someone had slid in beside him.

"Tony, I'm Jim Boy. How's it going?"

Tony let his mind clear for a moment before he turned toward the visitor. "Do I know you?" he asked.

"Me? Probably not, but I believe we know quite a lot about you," The visitor stated categorically as he opened up a racing form and brought it level with his face as if trying to hide his identity from others. "We've been watching you for the last couple years thinking that you would slow down on the bookmaking, maybe even get out of the business altogether."

"I don't know what you are talking about, Mr. Boy or Jim Boy, whoever you are."

"Do you remember last year when the police busted your mobile home? They confiscated your phones, beer, cash and notebooks, and then threw you in jail for a couple of days. My family thought that would surely put you out of business. In fact, I was the one who called the police. I told them we were neighbors who were suspicious gambling was taking place in our neighborhood. Then when I saw the report of the bust on the six o'clock news I thought, "That's it. Tony will never be able to run a bookmaking business in this state again. He's out of business for good!

"But by the time you got out of jail, your phones were reconnected and you were back in business. Consequently it doesn't look like you're going away. So with that in mind, we want you to join our organization, and then we will both prosper."

"I'm listening," Tony said while still looking up at the drifting clouds, but now he saw sports cars in the clouds.

"In addition to bookmaking, we have connections in New Orleans to first-hand cocaine. It arrives in a tanker at the port in pure form, and that's where we pick it up. You seem to have connections in central Arkansas, and we believe your network can successfully distribute our product. You interested?" Jim Boy asked.

Now with eyes glazed over, Tony casually leaned back while still looking at the sky imagining dollar signs embedded in the clouds. He grinned as the feeling of hitting a major trifecta swept over him.

Gulpha Gorge Park is located only a couple of miles outside of downtown Hot Springs. The campsites there are nestled in a canyon formed by two mountain ridges one-half mile apart. One of the thermal springs that made Hot Springs, Arkansas famous forms a creek that flows through the canyon.

Gulpha Gorge campgrounds were full that time of year with pop-up campers and Winnebago's populating the park. With the advent of spring, the campsite literally exploded with color. Dogwood trees spotted the mountainside in both pink and white blossoms while daffodils and jonquils alike lined the pathways. The sweet smell of honeysuckle always permeated the air that time of year as the babbling creek running through the campsite epitomized the serenity of the area. When darkness hit, raccoons could be found digging through the trash cans around the campsites where the creek flowed over basketball-sized boulders.

"I wonder what they're dreaming about," thought Freeway as he looked out at the row of multi-colored campers and tents lined up on the sequence of campsite pads. Probably dreaming about a higher interest rate on their certificates of deposit or other investments he thought. What a simple life they must have. They're probably retired from IBM or Wal-Mart, and currently trying to recapture all that lost time from having worked around the clock for the last twenty or thirty years.

"Thank God that's not me," he muttered to himself, realizing in about thirty minutes his dreams were going to start to come true, one-hundred thousand dollars in bulk cocaine. Coke that Tony and he would cut, bag, and sell for maybe ten times the original value on the streets! "Yes, our dreams are just about to become a reality," Freeway obsessed, while mentally rehearsing the plan step-by-step. We'll stash the cocaine in twenty different locations and then hit high schools, colleges, and back alleys."

"We need to find the fraternity that thinks they are too cool for school; they'll be a major purchaser of the coke. The students' parents who are footing the college bill will always send another hundred or two for a school project," Freeway thought out loud, while mentally working through his plan of attack, "The back alley is different. A white man selling cocaine in the ghetto simply won't fly. We need to recruit a runner or two. Pimps are always game for coke to get their ladies to work double time. In sixty days and there'll be enough sold to pay Jim Boy in full, then every sale after that is pure profit."

***

Tony would be delivered $100,000 of raw cocaine, and 60 days later, Tony would pay Jim Boy $200,000. The profit above that would be split 60/40 between Tony and Freeway. Tony knew he would end up with close to a half-million once the dealing was completed. No doubt this was the deal of a lifetime. Tony knew his ship had come in.

***

Freeway glanced down at his watch and smiled thinking it would take him twenty or thirty years to scrimp and save enough money just so he could go camping every now and then. Now in sixty days he'd have enough money to do anything he wanted.

An amphitheater was located in the back part of the campsite. On holidays the city sometimes had concerts or storytelling for the campers. However, tonight it was being used as a drop spot. Freeway made his way to the last row of the amphitheater. He sat on the exact spot where Jim Boy had instructed. His eyes blinked with every beat of his heart and triggered a throb between his eyes and ears. Beads of sweat formed on his upper lip, causing him to wonder if he had taken his blood pressure medicine that day. He looked at his watch then up at the stars, "I know I have the right night, and midnight was the time, but where is he?" Freeway said out loud to no one.

Freeway somehow thought it was lighter now than it had been an hour ago. Even though there was no moon to illuminate the area, the stars were bright. Some animal made a noise like a screen door opening and closing. He found three big – or little dippers – but couldn't decide if they were actually catching the water or pouring it back out into the galaxy. Then suddenly the screen door stopped, and the only audible sound was the beating of his heart. The rhythm amplified; Freeway noticed movement in his shirt throbbing in unison to the same tempo. Staring at the stage of the amphitheater and beyond into the shadows, he spied a figure. In the dark he couldn't tell if it was looking directly at him or in another direction entirely. He could only make out the contours of a human body, noticeably larger than the average person. As he thought about what could possibly go wrong, his nervousness escalated. What if there was more than one of them? What if he was being double-crossed? What if they were planning to beat him – or even kill him – then throw him in the creek?

He wondered if he should have had Tony come with him. He couldn't help thinking, "What the hell am I doing out here in the middle of the night?"

Then the shadow on the stage of the amphitheater moved toward him. As it grew larger, Freeway considered running, but his legs were frozen as his eyes followed the figure. Slowly, the shadow became a person; small, dressed in jeans and a plain red flannel shirt, hiking boots and a large backpack. It was a girl, and she looked as if she had just hiked over the top of North Mountain, but Freeway wasn't sure if this was his connection or not.

What had Jim Boy said? "Stay on the last row of the amphitheater and one of my boys will drop off the bag at your feet. Try to make it look natural, and whatever you do, don't botch the drop."

She had a natural look about her. If Freeway had been guessing, he would say she had grown up in Colorado and was reared by rich parents. Her blonde ponytail stuck out the back of her Kansas City

Royals baseball hat, and there was a noticeable bounce in her walk as she hurried up the stairs in his direction.

Freeway looked around to see if there might be someone else she was there to meet, but the place was empty. Not another soul in sight; she was here to see him!

"Honey, I missed you so much!" The mystery woman said, as she threw her arms around him and looked up toward his face and lips stating matter-of-factly, "Kiss me like the lover I want you to be, and *don't* say a word," she whispered as their lips met.

Freeway wasn't certain what was going on, but he knew how to follow orders. "What a kiss!" He thought. Had she mistaken him for someone else, or was she one of Jim Boy's helpers? Either way, this was a perk he hadn't counted on. For a moment, he was once again glad that Tony wasn't there and that this dirty detail was left up to him and him alone.

As their lips parted, they continued to embrace. She whispered in his ear again, "We never know if someone else is watching. The dope is in my backpack. Walk toward the bathhouse on the left, and we will split up there. I really hope no one has seen us."

Freeway carried her backpack to the bathhouse door as if he were a gentleman saying, "I'll wait for you in the truck." He toted the dope to his truck and laid it on the floorboard of the cab. He glanced around, and there was no one in sight, neither a sound nor a light.

"Should I drive off?" he pondered. I have the cocaine, and no one has seen us. Then as if skipping second gear he thought, "It's late at night. Maybe this young lady would like to get to know me a little better." After all, that kiss was still very fresh in his mind and thus controlling his thoughts.

If luck was lady tonight then Freeway felt lucky in this moment. He reached into the glove box for a bottle of mouthwash. It had been several hours, ten beers, and a pack of cigarettes since he had brushed his teeth. His typical stash of grooming items included: gum, mints, spray-on deodorant, and aftershave. He believed these simple sundries could cover up the worst of the male.

Looking at himself in the rear-view mirror, his blood pressure instantly shot straight up at the first sounds of the deafening *pow, pow, pow* of the racking of the pipes. It was the undeniable sound of a big Harley Davidson motorcycle. The noise amplified as it emanated from within the bathhouse. Freeway jerked his head in all directions at once, and out of the corner of his eye, he saw a dark figure come blasting out of the bathhouse wearing bulky clothing, a black helmet and a black face shield.

Giving no thought to how much noise she made, first gear wound tight and shifted into second. Then the front wheel rose off the ground at least 10 inches. The bike shifted into third and suddenly only a tail light could be seen. The silence of the night slowly recaptured the campsite. Dreams of what could have been just moments earlier still lingered in Freeway's thoughts as the scene oddly reminded him of an R.V. cemetery. He was numb.

As he lit another cigarette, he looked around without moving his head. He didn't know exactly why he was waiting or for that matter how long. After all Tony hadn't told him. Following another four or five cigarettes, Freeway decided to head for his apartment.

The plan had been to drive by Tony's mobile home and honk the horn in order to signal that the drop had been successful. When he pulled out of the Gulpha Gorge campsite and back onto the highway, a blaring horn rang out. He cut the wheels of the truck hard to the right, barely getting out of the way of the speeding vehicle: a Dodge Ram with a Rebel flag flowing haphazardly from a broom handle that was mounted to the middle of the cab. Several boys sat in the back of the truck bare chested. They were clearly intoxicated.

"Hey, get the hell off the road, you burnt-out hippy!" one of the boys yelled out as they sped past him.

"Damn, I had better start paying attention," he thought to himself as he eased back onto the road. His thinking had become clear now. He couldn't afford to get in a car wreck with the backpack full of cocaine. After all the last thing he wanted was to spend the next twenty years being somebody's wife down at Tucker State Penitentiary.

As he rounded the first curve, he saw a reflection on the side of the road. It was the Harley. The driver – who was fully clothed in black leather – still had the helmet in place. Freeway's headlights shot a reflection from the chrome as he pulled off the side of the road behind the Harley and the lucky lady.

"Well, well, well," Freeway said thinking out loud. "This lady must want to test out the shocks on my truck."

He turned off the headlights, took the last cigarette out of the pack, and tapped it on the dashboard. It could have been to either pack down the tobacco or to buy some extra time while he decided what his next move might be, but it didn't take long. The lucky lady pulled off her helmet and shook out her curls. Her shoulder length blonde hair spilled out over the collar of her black leather jacket. She then flashed Freeway a smile that showed dazzling white, perfect teeth.

Giving her the nod of approval, and a look that twenty years ago would have melted a young maiden's heart, he motioned for her to come to the truck.

The lucky lady unzipped her jacket as she sauntered up to the window. Freeway tilted his head backwards, to where it rested comfortably on the seat behind him the moment he saw her put her right hand down the front of her pants. His eyes closed as a slight smile traced across his lips. He never saw the pistol come out of a hidden pocket in the lining of her pants or the first shot that struck him above his left eye. His head jolted back on impact as its contents covered the ceiling and passenger window with a mixture of blood and brains. Then the second round unmercifully penetrated the side of his neck, leaving his jugular vein spewing like a fire hose.

CHAPTER 5
LOST AND NOT FOUND

Tony paced the floor between the kitchen window and the television set. A view through the kitchen window allowed him to see headlights at least 6 blocks away. In between the pacing, he paused to look at the television set, which was tuned to a local station.

"Where the hell is he?" Tony shouted as he threw his drink at the brick fireplace. Glass, ice, and good whiskey flew in all directions.

"How could I have trusted that idiot with my shipment of cocaine? I shouldn't have trusted anyone, including my own mother with this drop!"

Tony started to pace again, his face scrunched up, "You better not throw me under the bus Freeway!"

Suddenly he realized he was talking to himself loudly, "Okay, okay, don't get out of control. He'll be honking that horn any minute now," Tony said in an effort to rein in his anxiety.

***

"Breaker, breaker, good buddy, you got your ears on?" called a trucker over the CB radio. Tony kept a monitor tuned in to catch the local chatter. Usually the chatter was reporting where a cop shooting radar was parked ... but not tonight.

"You got the Mud Slinger here," another voice responded, as Tony listened in.

"This is the Donut Maker here, and I've just passed through the Gorge. We've got Smokies everywhere. It appears a wagon full of rednecks decided to take a look at the inside of an ol' boy's head out here."

"Well Donut Maker, do you think he's dead?"

"No thinking about it, Mud Slinger. I heard them say so when the bullet came out the back of that hippie's head. The crazy thing is they said it blew off his ponytail with about five inches of skull still attached. It hung on his gun rack."

"Well that's too bad, Donut Maker. Are you going to open up on time today, or are you running behind?"

"You can bet your booties we'll open on time. Too much money would be lost if I don't get that bakery up and going. I'm down and out, but I'll see you around four in the early morning."

"You can count on it," Mud Slinger replied; and then, the radio went silent.

***

After hearing the conversation between the owner of the local bakery and some other lonesome soul who couldn't sleep that night, emotions flooded over Tony. He moaned, "This was one of my best friends, shot by some rednecks. What does that mean? What about my cocaine? "Tony began fixing yet another drink as he pondered what had just happened.

He jumped with the first ring of the phone, wondering who could be calling at 3 o'clock in the morning. Looking at the caller ID, he only saw the word *unknown*.

"Hello," Tony answered as he dropped more ice into his glass.

"Tony, it's Jim Boy. I'm not going to say much on this phone except that you have something of mine and the 60 day countdown has started. I'll be looking for my two hundred thousand in exactly sixty days from today."

Click, the phone went dead.

CHAPTER 6
THE METER IS RUNNING: FAST

The sun dropped behind the leading edge of a low front that was going to bring some much needed rain. It had been about 6 weeks since the last downpour. The sky darkened even though it was still two hours from sunset. Tony dreaded going back to his mobile home, but he had to spend some time tonight calling his fair-weather friends and relatives.

The feeling of time slipping away consumed much of his day. With dark clouds rolling in from the west, there was an even darker cloud hanging over Tony's head now, and that cloud was Jim Boy. Jim Boy had his hand out wanting $200,000 cash in exchange for a load of cocaine that Tony has never seen.

***

Oaklawn Park was enjoying record daily attendance, and their handle (the amount of money bet on the races each day inside the park) was fifteen percent ahead of last year's figures. The casinos located in every border town of Arkansas had predicted that the money spent at Oaklawn would eventually be moving to them. This assumption had been correct for the first couple of years, but the Cella family had increased the amount of money the horse owners could win causing payoffs to the local bettors to substantially improve. Thus these two moves combined kept Oaklawn full of bettors wanting to watch world-class horses.

Tony was also having a record year in the bookmaking business. Two thousand a week in profits usually put Tony in a great frame of mind. During the day at the mobile home, he acted as if he was on top of the world. On any given day, ten to twelve gamblers loitered at the trailer, each of them with an average of several hundred dollars in his pocket. While it's true most gamblers typically think they can turn a couple of hundred dollars into a retirement plan, by the end of the day they left drunk and flat broke as two helpers answered the incoming phone calls in the converted bedroom from all corners of the state, assuring Tony had a thriving business.

In the three weeks since Freeway's death, Jim Boy had made it clear that the meter was running on Tony's debt for the two hundred thousand dollars in cash. Tony had promised Jim Boy he needed only sixty days to double the one hundred thousand dollars of raw cocaine, and anything over that would be Tony's while Freeway had advised Tony on the true street value of the drug. Together they figured they could cut it thin and end up with close to a million dollars.

Tony thought, "It would have been easy if all I had to do was sell the dope, but Freeway had to go and screw the project up. If he had only protected the cocaine..." his focus continued pushing him forward, "I'll have about half of what I owe Jim Boy in the safe-deposit box. Jim Boy would have to be happy with me and looking for another shipment of drugs to unload, and then I will be on Easy Street."

Terry Wallace, Oaklawn Park's announcer, was finishing his commentary on the last race when Tony said, "That's it guys, this day's over. I've enjoyed it, but I've got a headache and I'm ready to get the hell out of here. I feel like I'm coming down with something, so don't bother stopping by tomorrow. I'm taking the day off, because I need some rest."

"That's bullshit Tony," one of the gamblers named Rodney yelled back at him, "You took most of my money today, and I was planning on coming by tomorrow to win it back. I'm down a couple of thousand dollars to you over the last several weeks, and you're not shutting me down now. I don't give a shit if you're on your death bed," Rodney said emphatically, as his face turned red and the veins on each side of his head bulged. "You've got a business here, and I've been a player for the last two weeks! Now you're telling me you're quitting and closing up shop? That's a huge mistake."

"Thanks Rodney, you've helped me make up my mind. Here's a couple of hundred dollars for playing here, but I'll be gone in the morning," Tony stated calmly.

Then changing his tune a little, Rodney said, "This helps, but I'm still down," all while stuffing the money in his front pocket. "I'll go play the ponies with someone else."

His patron's cars left single file from the driveway. Finally, the trailer was empty except for Tony. He hadn't planned on shutting down, but he was getting used to the idea with every passing minute.

***

The shower felt great. Tony thought he could actually see his stress going down the drain along with the soapy water. He felt relieved about his decision to close the bookmaking operation. It would be quite a surprise for his regulars to find the door locked around 10:00am. That's when the first of what would eventually make up a dozen would arrive helping themselves to a beer in the refrigerator. Tony had an empty gallon-sized pickle jar on the cabinet next to the refrigerator for beer donations, but it never amounted to enough money to buy a six-pack, much less the next shipment of brew. That didn't bother Tony though, because he knew the consumption of beer took away all logic when it came to betting the horses. As the effects of alcohol began to take hold, the average bettor started loading up on a horse because of its name, mindless of whether the horse had a chance to win or not.

Fast was now the magic word. Tony had to come up with two hundred thousand dollars *fast* or Jim Boy would be a difficult person with which to deal. A cold chill came over Tony as he thought about the possible consequences.

CHAPTER 7
BRINGING IT TOGETHER STRAIGHT AND NARROW

Bradley graduated with a 3.5 GPA. In addition, he received All State Honors for being the best tailback in Southwest portion of Arkansas. He felt complete.

March 1st - three years before the death of Freeway - was a big day for the Lakeside Stampede. Bradley was signing a letter of intent to play football for the University of Central Arkansas Bears. Lakeside High had set up a table at center court in the field house. A capacity crowd there was listed at 6010, but today - with kids hanging off the rafters - the count would be closer to 7000. The signing ceremony would only last about five minutes, but the pep rally started an hour or so earlier. Each coach made a speech about how he had enjoyed coaching Bradley and what an asset he had been to the school as well as Hot Springs.

"I want to thank all of the fans who came out every Friday night to support the Stampede," Bradley stated. "The fans as well as the offensive line deserve the right to share in the glory and thrill of this moment. My success is their success. I plan on playing football at the University of Central Arkansas and after that I don't know." Bradley concluded with, "I love each of you, I love Lakeside, and…GO BEARS!"

During Bradley's second week of practice within the course of his junior year, he blew out his knee with an anterior cruciate ligament tear, tragically ending his hopes and dreams of football forever, but he graduated a semester early. It was easy to keep up with his classes and homework when he no longer had to spend his time running, keeping in shape, and attending practice every afternoon. He had majored in business with a minor concentration in insurance. UCA had been one of the few universities around who offered insurance as a minor.

The University always held a job fair at the end of each semester, and Bradley spent most of the morning going from booth to booth looking for a career on which he could build his future. Jerry Carter, the District Manager for the Premier Insurance Company of America, was busy putting his brochures and pamphlets away when Bradley stopped in front of his booth.

"Have you got any openings for a beat-up football has-been?" Bradley grinned, as he put out his hand to shake with Jerry Carter.

"Where's your hometown son?" Jerry asked.

"Hot Springs. Four years ago, every person in that town knew my face and my name, and wanted nothing more than to see me be successful. The only problem is they wanted my success to be on the football field, and I'm afraid that I've let them down."

"Hot Springs," Jerry commented, while raising his eyebrows and nodding with approval, "We need a branch office there. It's been my experience in life that when a town loves you they also want to see you become something better than your average Joe. They'll support you in areas other than football, because they have already invested in your success. If you get into the insurance business with the Premier Insurance Company of America, you'll be surprised how many townspeople will be there for you." Jerry Carter expressed, without taking his eyes off Bradley.

"Hot Springs remembers you as if it were yesterday, and with the proper training, you can't miss," was the last thing the District Manager said before Bradley was ready to hit the ground running.

The day after the first advertisement ran in the Hot Springs Sentinel Record, Bradley's insurance business took off as expected. He joined the Downtown Rotary Club and the Noon Lions Club. His phone began ringing off the hook, and Bradley started to build his insurance dynasty.

"It's great to be back in Hot Springs, and it's great to be a part of this fine community," became his new mantra, and he stated it as often as he could.

"Bradley I don't believe I've ever had an agency grow as fast as yours is growing," Jerry told him over lunch one day. "In fact, we need to do more training, but I hate to slow you down by making you sit through more classes. Instead just make sure you *dot every I and cross every T* on the applications, because I can't review each and every piece of paper as fast as you are."

Sitting in his office, Bradley picked up the phone by the second ring. "Premier Insurance Company, this is Bradley."

"I know I'm several months late in congratulating you on your new career, but I'm sure glad to have you back in town. This is Tony LaTour. You haven't forgotten me have you, Mr. Football Star?"

"Tony! Thanks for calling. What's up?"

"I've formed a small company with Ricky Alexander," Tony began explaining, "We're in charge of demographics for sporting events. Right at this moment we're working for both Oaklawn Park in Hot Springs and Kansas University in Lawrence, Kansas. We find out where the customers are coming from and then key that same information into the computer. Overall it's a pretty good set up.

"After the numbers are crunched, we know if their advertising is actually working or not. Then if it's not, we might suggest another geographical area in which to target their spending."

Bradley shrugged his shoulders wondering how that worked and laughed, "You always did like to make your living from off Oaklawn Park. Are you still booking the horse races?"

"No I gave that shit up a while back. I'm on the straight and narrow earning my money the legitimate way."

"I was sorry to hear about Freeway. They say he was shot and killed for no apparent reason. Do you know if the police have any leads on his death?"

"I don't think so," Tony replied, "but I'm still in a state of shock. Freeway was a friend of mine, but you know I didn't condone all he was doing. I've heard the police are closing the door on the investigation, so I guess we'll never know exactly what happened." Then shifting his focus rather quickly Tony said, "Bradley, I need to get with you in the next day or so to take out a life insurance policy on myself in order to protect my business."

Then Bradley replied, "Something as important as insuring your future earnings shouldn't wait Tony. Let's get together later today to get the paperwork going. Come by the office around five. I'll be wrapping up my day, and I can go over the details with you then," Bradley said crossing his fingers.

"I'll be there at five," Tony agreed. The phone call was done.

CHAPTER 8
"IN FORCE"

It had been several years since Bradley and Tony had last talked. Bradley had lost several hundred dollars betting with Tony. He always felt screwed on the bets. Once Tony told him he had arrived at the track too late to place the bet after Bradley's horse had won, but he was certain that Tony would have pocketed the money if the horse had lost.

Another time Bradley - even though he was a non-drinker - bought several bottles of wine from Tony and Freeway and then gave them to the offensive line. Once Bradley realized what the mark-up was on the wine, he couldn't believe it! He felt Tony had taken advantage of him and thought *one day he would get back at Tony*.

Now the shoe was on the other foot, and it was time to get his money back. Selling Tony a life insurance policy would put some commission back in Bradley's pocket. He couldn't help remembering an old saying his District Manager, Mr. Carter, had told him about doing business with people you don't like, "You don't have to have them over for chicken on Sunday afternoon to make a meal off of them."

***

The magnetic doorbell signaled Tony's arrival. "Hey, long time no see," Bradley remarked brandishing a warm smile from ear to ear with his hand outstretched to welcome Tony.

"Shit! Man you haven't aged a day since the last time I saw you," Tony said as he stared deeply into Bradley's eyes. "I used to live to watch you run with the football. You left defenders scattered around the field wondering what had just happened. I believe every time you scored a touchdown my bootlegging orders picked up. After all, a Friday night football game filled with a lot of scoring on the football field usually meant there'd also be a lot of scoring outside the stadium. But that's all behind me and ancient history now you know."

Primary Beneficiary

"Let me tell you what I have on my mind," stated Tony. "Do you remember Ricky Alexander? He was the right guard on the football team, and he dated Becky Boston."

"Sure, I remember Ricky. I always made certain that I stayed on the good side of my blockers. If the offensive line decided that a running back was getting too cocky and not appreciative of his blockers, they'd decide to miss a block or two, and that running back left the game on a stretcher," replied Bradley.

"Ricky Alexander..." I haven't even thought of his name since high school. Tell me again. What are you two doing?"

"Ricky lives in Kansas City now. Actually it's Lawrence, Kansas, about twenty minutes out of Kansas City. He's doing the same type of research at Kansas University that I do at Oaklawn Park. We contract with a sporting arena to help them with their marketing. I write down license plate numbers from Oaklawn, and Rickey does the same thing at Allen Field House, where the Kansas Jayhawks play basketball. We then put the numbers into a computer to crunch them, and the computer identifies what percentage of the attendees comes from which state and zip code. This way they know if they need to advertise in a particular city or state.

"We've been doing this kind of work for several months now, and it's time we protect each other's interests by covering the investments we've already made. This work is going so well, and it's so unique that we've had other schools contact us. We've already talked to Six Flags, so our business is sitting on a vibrating rocket, and the countdown to blast-off has already started.

"We use an accountant in Kansas City, and he told us we need something called Key Man insurance. He explained it usually costs an enormous amount of money - at least enormous to us - but if something happened to either of us, there would be enough money to keep the business in operation."

Bradley could smell a big sale coming, and the timing couldn't be more perfect. The Premier Insurance Company always had trips and contests going to some exotic place for their top producers. On the last report from his home office, Bradley was named among the top ten of all agents in Arkansas. If he was reading Tony correctly, he could start working on his tan tomorrow.

Ricky will be down in a couple of weeks, but he wanted me to get these policies taken care of this week. We are applying for another loan, and the bank wants to be certain that we have enough coverage to pay off the note in the event something happened to one of us. Ricky and I have both already signed a Power of Attorney stating that each of us has the authority to sign for the other on any project that involves our business," said Tony.

"It certainly sounds like you two have done your homework," Bradley stated, as he began hitting the keys on his computer.

"In a Buy-Sell Agreement," Bradley began his presentation, "the business owners must first decide how much their business is actually worth in terms of dollars and cents. For instance, if you were to settle on $100,000 - and in this case there are two owners - each half of the business would be worth $50,000. That is the amount that each of you is entitled to if the business is either sold or dissolved in the event of an untimely death. Therefore, if either of the owners were to die, the survivor would receive the full amount of which one-half would be used to purchase the deceased partner's share from his spouse or other family members. This is all taken care of with the use of Life Insurance."

"Have you met with an attorney to draw up the Buy-Sell Agreement?" Bradley asked with his fingers crossed underneath his desk.

"Sure. We did so last week, but our attorney hasn't given us the final draft yet," Tony remarked while lighting a cigarette. "It's okay if I send you a copy later isn't it? I simply don't have it with me."

"I'm really not sure if it is or not," Bradley replied, trying to remember if that had been covered during a training class he'd already had with District Manager Jerry Carter. "It won't prevent us from doing the paperwork and getting the applications sent off to the company. I'll make a note of that and check with the home office tomorrow to see exactly what needs to be completed and sent in."

"Then the insurance doesn't go into force for several weeks," a visibly agitated Tony blurted out while scooting to the edge of his seat. A long ash from his cigarette fell on Bradley's desk, but neither of them looked at it.

After a few more tense moments, Tony casually leaned back in his chair and shook his head in disgust while saying, "Look Bradley, I know you're new in the insurance business and have probably never written this type of policy, or at least one as large as we need..." Tony was now talking in a much calmer, controlled voice.

"I've already spoken with two other companies in town, and they were going to get everything completed and in force immediately. In fact, I was talking to them before I found out you were even in the business. I do understand if this is out of your league." Tony was reading Bradley's face like a book.

"You probably need to stick to insuring babies and old cars. Why don't we call it a night, and I'll see one of the other agents first thing in the morning and get this completed?" Tony pushed back out of his chair and started to stand.

I'm blowing the best opportunity for the biggest sale of my career, Bradley thought to himself. Damned if I'm going to let this chance get away. Leaning forward and looking Tony straight in the eye, Bradley explained, "Tony, I'm taking care of your policies tonight. If I need any additional information then I'll let you know."

Then Tony settled back down and asked, "If I sign the application and give you money, are these policies in force?"

"Sure, they are in force. As soon as you lift the pen from the paper, you're covered," Bradley responded affirmative.

"How can I be certain?" Tony was leaning forward. Bradley and Tony's faces were only inches apart.

"Because I carry insurance to protect me against any mistakes," said Bradley, who still couldn't believe that Tony was sitting in his office acting like some big shot needing a large policy. "For the same reasons that doctors carry malpractice insurance, I carry error and omissions insurance, because I occasionally do big cases, even bigger than what you need. This time it was Bradley who leaned back in his chair suddenly feeling like the man in charge again.

"Tony, if I say you're covered then you can bet your boots you're covered. Now let's fill out the paperwork and go have a beer."

"Bradley, I only have a few concerns and even fewer questions," Tony said as he lit up another cigarette. He had also straightened his back to sit as tall in his chair as possible and leaned slightly forward. "Ricky and I have poured our life savings into this business opportunity, and if you fuck up the insurance by doing something wrong, your career in this field will be over. If these policies are out of your league, I want you to be man enough to refer me to a more experienced agent."

Tony's voice became a whisper, "I need these policies done right and I'm coming to you as a friend, not because I think you are a great agent."

Bradley could feel the veins on the side of his forehead bulge as his true feelings for Tony began to emerge. Deep down, he always resented Tony's attitude even back in high school. Tony always had a money clip stretched to the limit with large bills saying he could get anything money could buy for his customers whether that be beer, whiskey or drugs. Rumor had it that once Tony even took money to have someone beat up for dating the wrong girl, and that Tony could set up hookers for a night if a person had enough money. How dare this street punk come into his office and belittle him! Didn't he know Bradley was one of the top writers of life insurance in Arkansas? Besides that, he wasn't about to let him walk out of there so he could go make another agent's day, Bradley thought as he tried to regain his composure.

"I've got the expertise, Tony. The real question is do you have the money necessary to bind these policies tonight?" Bradley asked raising his eyebrows while still making full eye contact with Tony. "Hey big shot, I'd say the balls in your court now!"

Tony's cold stare revealed no emotions whatsoever as he remarked, "Run the numbers and let's find out."

Then Bradley turned to his computer and started asking questions, "Tony, this first quote will be on you. Are you twenty-six yet?"

"I'm twenty-seven and a non-smoker," he answered while putting out another cigarette.

"That's right, I forgot that you had to repeat the second grade because you couldn't spell mother," Bradley knew that when other students had foolishly brought up the failed grade, they ended up in a fist fight. But not this time though, because Bradley had Tony eating out of his hand. Great! He's a year older than I remembered, plus a smoker has a much higher monthly premium than a non-nicotine user. I'm going to make more money on this than I thought.

"Exactly how large a policy do you need?" Bradley asked as he typed $100,000 into his computer out of habit. Most people thought

$100,000 was what they needed, so he had been automatically using that figure for practically everyone who came into the office.

Tony sat quietly. He looked at Bradley showing no evidence of emotion on his face, and then he looked at a piece of paper lying on the desk while Bradley continued staring at his computer screen for a few more seconds. Then Bradley turned to look at Tony making certain he'd heard his question.

"Ricky and I have determined that our business is worth $1.2 million at this time, so we each need $600,000. I need to get the policy on myself insuring my life for $600,000 with Ricky being named the primary beneficiary."

Bradley's fingers froze still on the keyboard while his throat seemed to instantly dry out and tighten. The dollar amounts began spinning in his mind. Can I write a policy that large? Did he actually say $1.2 million? Breathe Bradley, he thought as if coaching himself through this moment. Get it done, stay cool and by all means don't let Tony see the excitement starting to swell.

"Tony, the first month's premium for your policy is going to be $850." His voice was slightly higher than normal. "How about a beer, I think I'm going to have one."

"Sure, why not?"

Bradley had never drank anything stronger than diet coke when he was in the middle of a sale, but he felt things were about to get out of hand, and he didn't want to lose a shot at policies this large.

Bradley was doing the math ... with the sale of $850 for each policy or $1,700 each month in premiums he had just made about $10,000 dollars on this sale. He knew he was putting some distance between himself and the second-place producer in the contest to the islands.

Tony looked straight into Bradley's eyes. A silence consumed the room as Bradley glanced around wondering what had been said last. Had Tony asked a question?

Tony leaned forward and whispered, "Bradley, I asked *where I sign*? You do remember what to do when someone asks that question?"

"Sure, but you didn't say anything about the $1,700. Are you certain the monthly amount won't be a burden to pay?" Bradley asked.

Tony relaxed leaning back in his chair as he chuckled, "I don't believe that will be a problem at all. I feel better now that I know if something happens to me, Ricky will get enough money to buy my half of the business. Now my family is protected if I should die, and Ricky wouldn't have to sell the business. After all that's what all of this is about, isn't it? Don't tell me you're only thinking about your commission?"

"Come on Tony, commissions are paid for jobs well done. Yeah I get paid for what I do, but the most important part of this transaction is that you're covered. Insurance is the only product that can give you total peace of mind. Think about how great you'll feel once Ricky gets his policy with you being the primary beneficiary. As it stands today, if Ricky were to die you'd have to borrow $600,000 to buy out Ricky's half or else sell the business outright, but now Ricky's wife, Becky, will get the first $600,000 and you'll get whatever's left ... even if it's only fifty bucks."

"Yeah I know, but Ricky won't be in town for a couple of months." Tony was looking depressed, and then all of a sudden he brightened and shouted, "Hey, I got a great idea!"

Bradley stopped typing to look at Tony.

"I'm going to give Ricky a call first thing in the morning and tell him to go see Jim Fender. Jim has been one of the most successful insurance agents in Lawrence, Kansas for the past twenty years. Jim can have that policy written and in place by noon."

Bradley's heart sank. With Tony's policy written, I'm probably going to be in first place on the Cayman Island promotion, but if I could also get the policy covering Ricky, I could call Susan and tell her to start tanning. Her super husband and super insurance agent had just hit a home run.

Tony looked at his watch and said, "Bradley, we need to wrap this up. I've enjoyed the conversation and doing business, but I have to drive to New Orleans tonight, and it will be several weeks before I'm back in town. I've got about ten minutes, and then I have to head for the door."

Bradley's heart stopped as he thought about losing out on Ricky's policy and possibly the Cayman Island trip in the process. Spinning his chair around to face his credenza behind his desk, he pulled out two applications and said, "Didn't I hear you say that Ricky had given you the *Power of Attorney* to sign his name for the good of your business?"

"Yes, but are you positive that when I sign Ricky's name on this application, the policy is bound and in force?"

"That's correct," Bradley stated emphatically as he rushed to get the papers in position.

"Ricky is still twenty-six and he has never smoked."

Bradley quickly figured up the premium for Ricky and stated, "Ricky's is cheaper, being a year younger and nicotine-free. It's $600 each month." He pushed a few buttons on the Casio calculator and said, "I need a check for $1,450 and a few signatures, then you'll be on your way to New Orleans. Both policies are bound, in force, and both you and Ricky are covered."

"Let's do cash," Tony suggested, "and I will need a receipt and a short note explaining what I bought. I'll fax Ricky the note tomorrow," he said pulling out a wad of one hundred dollar bills from his pocket.

"No problem," said Bradley, as he started writing a summary on his letterhead ... *Purchased today, a life policy for $600,000 on the life of Tony LaTour with the primary beneficiary named Ricky Alexander, and another life policy covering the life of Ricky Alexander for $600,000 with the primary beneficiary named Tony LaTour. I've collected the first month's premium totaling $1,450 for both policies. The coverage is now in force.*

"Tony, for the sake of saving time, I'm not going to mess with the Power of Attorney thing. I'm just going to add to the letter that both Mr. LaTour and Mr. Alexander were both present."

"Yeah, that's fine with me, and it'll probably save some paperwork."

Bradley handed the signed receipt to Tony, who read it aloud and slowed his speech once he got to the section that clearly stated *both parties were present*. Looking back at Bradley, Tony said, "Bradley, I can't begin to tell you how lucky I am to have someone like you in the insurance business."

Then Bradley said thanks while thinking to himself, you think you're lucky? I just won a trip to the Cayman Islands.

CHAPTER 9
FRATERNIZING

Ricky Alexander couldn't believe the basketball game was tied at halftime. The *Lawrence Journal-World* had picked the Jayhawks as a sixteen point favorite, but most of the followers of college basketball also knew that when the Kansas State Wildcats came to town, the game was always close and never boring. This game had everyone on the edge of their seats. Roy Williams, head basketball coach at the University of Kansas, had suspended two of his starters for their involvement with a local sports agency.

Coach Williams heard through the grapevine that Sean Jackson and Freddy McKee had been the guests of Gary Westerman at the local strip joint called The Flamingo. The locals simply called it The Dirty Bird, which was much more fitting. It was a great hangout for the fraternity boys of KU. The pitchers of beer were cheap, and the girls who worked were paid by tips only so this kept the overhead down, with Westerman not having to pay any of his workers. Even though Coach Williams didn't allow any alcohol consumption or smoking of any type from any of his players, on occasion he was willing to look the other way. But this was different ... for the National Collegiate Athletic Association (NCAA) states that to lobby or court any player who is still attending and competing in college athletics was not only unethical, it was forbidden. Coach Williams might have dismissed the knowledge as rumor, but Jackson and McKee's pictures had now been printed in the Sunday paper alongside the sports agent and three of the local strippers as they were leaving the club. Looking the other way could trigger an NCAA investigation, and at best KU would be fined, and the basketball team could lose a scholarship or two.

Losing a scholarship can result in not recruiting a really valuable player for the future, so Coach Williams called a press conference at Allen Fieldhouse on Monday before the game with Kansas State on Tuesday. The rumors had been flying in all directions. Some of the fans who thought they knew Coach well enough to second guess his reactions said that he would kick the two players off the squad.

There was also a group who knew how important winning the Big 12 Conference was to the Jayhawks' future in recruiting. After all, if a team is on its way down and hasn't won their conference in a year or two, a top recruit may decide to attend another college. Coach Williams needed these players in the post-season tournaments.

Another group was even saying that he might announce his leaving the Jayhawks and taking over the North Carolina Tar Heels. Dean Smith had retired and Roy had been his assistant for many years before landing his current job with the University of Kansas. Coach Williams had been the recruiter who was credited with landing Michael Jordan for the Tar Heels.

But not on this day ... Coach Williams assembled the media, fans and local wonderers in front of the main entrance of Allen Fieldhouse. At precisely 12:00 pm, Coach Williams walked to the podium and announced, "It saddens me to inform you that two of our players, Sean Jackson and Freddy Williams, broke a major team rule this past week. They were out past curfew, and for this violation, they will sit out the game against the Kansas State Wildcats. All of you have heard the rumors in addition to the curfew violation, but in my opinion they were simply rumors, and I will not make a comment speculating on rumors. We will miss them in our quest to keep the string of home games victories intact, but I will not allow the team rules to be broken without proper punishment. It is my wish that we fill Allen Fieldhouse to the rafters on Tuesday, and let's send those Wildcats back down Interstate 70 with their tails between their legs. Thank you." With that said, the press conference was over.

CHAPTER 10
SOUNDS OF SILENCE

Thousands of Kansas fans filed out of the complex shaking their heads and cursing under their breaths, "How could we let this game get away from us?" Still others knew that Coach should have let Jackson and Williams play while simultaneously saying and thinking to themselves, "This game was far too important to make them sit on the bench."

Ricky Alexander was always one of the last to leave the Fieldhouse. He liked listening to the sounds of silence slowly reclaiming the massive old building where just minutes earlier a crowd roared loud enough to drown out a 747 jet.

Ricky walked slowly past the glass trophy case with its pictures of All-Americans who had once played sports at the University of Kansas, among other such greats as Gayle Sayers, Willie Pless, Danny Manning, and Wilt Chamberlain. As he stepped outside of the building, Ricky immediately felt the north wind slap the side of his face. He turned his back and flipped up the collar of his London Fog overcoat, the stars appeared so close he wanted to wave his hand through the air to see if he could touch one. With the temperature hovering around 12° Ricky had to keep his hands in his pockets to keep them from getting frostbitten. He walked across the front lawn of Allen Fieldhouse, grass crunching under each step, to Lot 4 across the street. There in the corner of the parking lot was his favorite parking space, usually well-lit by the overhead street light. *My street light is out,* he thought to himself. *I know it was working when I arrived, I wonder what the hell happened to it. Shit, it's dark out here, but look at those stars. I've never seen them brighter.* Ricky's right hand, deep in his pocket was staying warm, while simultaneously holding onto his car keys tightly.

Looking up at the sky, he didn't see the shadow wearing tight fitting, black clothing, black boots, and a ski mask slip quietly in step behind him. The assassin – with the force and skill of a martial arts expert – executed a right-handed military salute into Ricky's larynx, breaking his windpipe in the process. Then with his left elbow between Ricky's shoulder blades, the intruder clasped his hands together on the left side of Ricky's head and stepped backward with his right foot. In one swift move, he'd managed to put Ricky in a sitting position, thus pushing his head forward and stopping the flow of both wind and blood to the brain. In sixty seconds, Ricky was dead. This was the same maneuver taught to every Marine in hand-to-hand combat training.

CHAPTER 11
CUT AND DRIED

"What a week! I've written three homeowners policies, six car policies, and two huge life insurance policies. I was born to sell insurance!"

The phone started ringing while Bradley was stuffing the applications into the large, gold-colored envelope that gets mailed into the company at the end of each week.

The phone was on its third ring when Bradley snatched it from the cradle and said, "Premier Insurance Company."

"Hey Bradley, I'm glad I caught you. It's Tony."

Bradley stiffened up and gritted his teeth together, wishing he hadn't answered the phone. *I have to get caller ID for this office,* Bradley thought. *If Tony backs out on the life insurance policies, I can kiss the big trip goodbye.*

"Hi Tony, did you call hoping to get more insurance on you and Ricky?" Bradley said, thinking it was worth a try.

"That's a thought, but I'm afraid it's too late to raise the coverage," Tony's voice was soft and barely audible. He also sounded nervous, jumpy. "Bradley, when I was writing you a check for the life insurance policies, you said we were covered. Are you sure?"

"Tony, of course I'm sure. I may be a relatively new agent in the insurance field, but I've done my homework and I know what I'm doing. Why? Do you want me to notify a bank or someone else about these policies?"

Bradley still had the applications and premium on his desk. If Tony asked for the money back, Bradley had decided that he would tell Tony that he had mailed everything into the company and it was too late to back out. Mentally, Bradley had already started packing for the trip to the islands, so he was not about to let Tony get his money back.

Primary Beneficiary

"I'm afraid I've got some tragic news. Ricky Alexander was killed in an auto accident last night."

There was at least 15 seconds of total silence. A cloud of impending disaster began to envelope Bradley. His eyes rolled back in his head, and his jaw dropped slightly as he gasped for a breath of air while he quickly hung up the telephone. The sound of his ink pen hitting the floor startled him back to reality. He offered up a quick prayer that he was hallucinating and had not actually spoken to Tony. The office was quiet except for the deafening throbbing of the clock that sat on the corner of the credenza behind his desk.

Bradley realized that the ringing in his ears was actually the phone and the same object capable of changing his day into an immediate disaster, maybe causing his short career to come to an abrupt end. The mistakes he'd made in writing the policy on Ricky were pelting him now as if it was a hard, drowning rain. He shouldn't have completed the application or collected the premium with Ricky not being present. Bradley knew in the back of his mind that the application had to be signed personally by Ricky to be valid. But who would have thought that Ricky would die before the policy was even sent to the company?

The ringing grew louder and louder while Bradley sat in a daze. In slow motion, he raised the phone to his ear.

"Hello?" Bradley questioned.

"It's Tony. Man, are you okay?" He sounded ever so slightly frustrated.

Short of breath and choosing his words carefully, Bradley spoke into the phone, "It's not as cut and dried as you might think; I'm not absolutely certain that Ricky's policy was completed correctly."

"Don't pull that shit with me, insurance man. You've told me twice now that we were covered, and I want to inform you that I recorded our phone conversation from night before last and I'm also recording this one." Tony's voice was cold, cutting through Bradley's heart as he gasped for air once again and collapsed back into his leather executive chair.

"I want to know right now what I have to do to collect my money."

"I'm not for certain. I've never had a death claim before. I believe all I need to do is contact the company and they will send you a check."

"I'm counting on it going that smooth."

"Tony, don't tell anyone that Ricky wasn't here to complete and sign the application."

"Don't worry."

The phone, again, was silent.

CHAPTER 12
TRIFECTA

Tony slept for a couple of hours. His mobile home looked as if the Lakeside Stampede had held a victory party inside the trailer. Beer cans covered the round coffee table in the middle of the living room. Any space on the table not occupied by cans had ashtrays that mounded in the middle. The stale smell of polluted air won the battle for supremacy over the continuously running air conditioner. It would take a woman's touch and two or three days with the windows open to get the trailer back to being livable. Tony summoned two or three of the young women that were constantly hanging around, and got them on that job.

After Tony showered and dressed, he went alone to Coy's Steakhouse. Coy's had been in business for about 60 years and was a time-honored tradition with the horse-racing crowd. When one had a winning day at the races, it was customary to suggest Coy's, known for its aged beef and warm crackers fresh from the oven. High rollers, or at least the people who wanted to give the impression they were affluent, were drawn to the establishment like moths to a flame, and it was customary to pick up the tab for the table.

He decided that tonight was a night to celebrate. Within the next couple of weeks he'd be receiving a check from the Premier Insurance Company for $600,000. This would be enough money to pay Jim Boy the two hundred thousand he owed for the cocaine that Freeway had let get away from him. Then he'd still have a cool four hundred thousand dollars to stash away in some untraceable account. He'd live on the interest until inflation eventually forced him back to work.

Tony rolled the dice and had come up a winner. Although he'd lost his friend, Freeway, and he'd taken a huge risk with Ricky and the life insurance policy, tonight everything was coming together, making it feel as if he'd suddenly hit the Triple Crown Trifecta.

David L. Tackett

Tony shook his head in disbelief as he thought back about his meeting with Bradley to take out the life insurance policy on Ricky. Tony had planned on getting a $250,000 policy that would pay off Jim Boy and still give him $50,000. But when Bradley started throwing around large figures, Tony got caught up in it and had used the amount of six hundred thousand each to test him.

Bradley, having been a rookie salesman, started seeing plaques with his name in all capital letters proclaiming him the #1 Life Insurance Salesman in Arkansas. Bradley was an easy target for this part of the plan. A more experienced agent would have never written the policies without having met all of the proposed clients. Bradley had made the mistake of telling him that both he and Ricky were covered once the premiums were collected. Usually collecting money or premiums guarantee that a policy is bound and in force. Life insurance policies in that range of coverage can typically only be submitted to the company for review and underwriting. Premiums are never collected on policies with a face amount more than $500,000. Bradley had made some stupid mistakes during his short time in the insurance business, but never any as ridiculous as the policies he wrote on Tony and Ricky.

Tony had another insurance policy on himself which no one had known about. When he was at Bradley's office, Tony had a small recording device in his pocket, recording everything that was being said. He was especially proud of the part when Bradley explained that the coverage was in force, and both he and his error and omissions coverage had made it so. The day on which error and omission insurance was explained to Bradley was the day he proclaimed that he could not make a mistake that would not be covered by his company. If Bradley says it's covered, then by God it's covered. The recollection made Tony smile.

Bradley even leaned over the desk to make certain that Tony heard him loud and clear. All the while, Tony had thought, "I hear you brother, and I'm recording every word just in case *you* don't remember."

"May I bring you a cocktail?" the waitress asked.

As he looked around Coy's Steakhouse, he replied, "Glen Livet on the rocks."

CHAPTER 13
LYING AND TRYING

"I'm never going to get out of here," Jerry said aloud to himself as the phone started ringing. "Let me check the caller ID, and if it's not Barbara or my boss, then I'm not answering it!"

Bradley. He must be working late like Jerry. Since new agents tend to have all kinds of questions, he answered, "Premier Insurance Company, Jerry Carter speaking."

"It's Bradley, I've got some bad news. There's been an accident, and I've got a big claim." Bradley's voice sounded in desperate need of confirmation that everything was going to be all right.

"Bradley, take a deep breath. You've had claims before. Settle down and start from the top," Jerry said as he tried to calm Bradley. "Did someone's house catch on fire or was there a car wreck?"

"It was an auto accident Jerry, a single vehicle accident that happened last night in Lawrence, Kansas." Bradley's voice was breaking up on the phone from losing control of his emotions. "It's bad Jerry, but I did everything right by the book." Bradley was lying, desperately trying to convince himself that he'd made honest mistakes while thinking at the same time *God, I hope I haven't screwed up my career!*

Bradley was smoking a cigarette as he stared at the life insurance applications on Ricky and Tony still lying on his desk with the sweat beading on his forehead, his hands shaking with the cigarette paper wet from the sweat on his fingers. It had been about an hour and a half since Bradley received the phone call from Tony reporting the death of his business partner, Ricky Alexander.

"It was a fluke accident Bradley," Tony had said. "Ricky was apparently coming home from the University of Kansas basketball game last night when he lost control of his vehicle. He was on Clinton Parkway driving too fucking fast, acting like an idiot. He left the road and hit head-on with a sandstone statue of a buffalo standing in prairie grass at the beginning of a park. He had his seat belt on, but the police said he went forward with his throat hitting the steering wheel, shattering his wind pipe and possibly breaking his neck."

"I'm sorry to hear that you had a client killed in an auto accident," Jerry replied, "but in terms of claims cost, it's not going to be that costly to the company. We will pay whatever medical bills are related to the accident, such as the ambulance or the fire truck going to the scene. Of course, we will pay for the vehicle he wrecked if he had collision coverage. What kind of car was he driving?" Jerry could hear Bradley's breath over the phone and a rhythmic tapping noise, which was Bradley's knee shaking and hitting the underside of his desk.

"I don't know what he was driving. I didn't have the car insured."

"Keep talking, because I'm not following you." Jerry turned and hit the record button on his phone. He learned years ago that accurate documentation of everything said between himself and his agents was important. After all, an agent could say that he had not been properly trained and put the blame back on the manager if something went wrong with a claim.

CHAPTER 14
SOMETIMES, MOE WASN'T ALWAYS LUCKY

His dinner at Coy's was perfect. He even had Moe as his waitress. She was a cute lady who had worked forty years at Coy's and was known for telling the dirtiest jokes in town. This restaurant served a great meal, plus a comedy show when you were lucky enough to get Moe. Tony ordered the king cut of prime rib because, after all, in a few days he would be able to act and possibly live like a king once the proceeds from the life insurance policy found his address.

Tony arrived back at his mobile home around 10:00pm. He had always felt uneasy walking into his pitch-dark mobile home. For some unknown reason, the light switch was not located by the front door. He had to shuffle through the darkness and the living area to the kitchen before hitting the switch. From where he stood, he could see the red light on the answering machine with its rhythmic blinking. He flipped on the light switch, and his eyes surveyed the room coming to rest on the red, blinking light. In the cabinet above the stove, Tony found a half-empty bottle of Aberlour Scotch. With half-and-half scotch and Mountain Valley water, he pushed the button on the answering machine. The indicator reported three messages: the first was at 7:07pm but left no message; the second at 7:16pm, and still no message; and third was at 7:21pm, "Hi, Tony, it's Bradley. I'm not for certain that we'll pay off on this. Call me tomorrow at the office, and I'll go over the information about Ricky's policy with you."

His eyes instantly darted about the room in order to make certain he was the only one in the room to have heard the message.

Tony's lips parted showing his clenched teeth. A guttural noise sounding like a growl came out as he flipped the light switch to the off position. Once again he stood in total darkness.

CHAPTER 15
THE GOOD OL' DAYS

It was a long drive to Lawrence, Kansas from Hot Springs, but the windshield time accomplished one thing for Bradley: it gave him time to think and unwind. In the safety of his seven year old Town Car, Bradley welcomed the solitary feeling that came over him. The car's phone had interrupted his serenity moments before when Stacy called to chitchat. He and Stacy had been married sixteen months earlier in a ceremony that rivaled Prince Charles' and Lady Diana's wedding.

"Honey, I'm running out of my cell phone area in a few miles so I can't talk now, and it will be a couple of hours before I get through the Ouachita Mountains and get service again," Bradley had informed Stacy. "So don't bother trying to get in touch with me. I'll call you back later tonight." As he hung up the cell he thought how good it was to get her off the phone as fast as he had. She'd been on his ass about money ever since he'd blown out his knee.

Bradley was thankful that they had not run up a lot of bills and debt thinking that a signing bonus and a lucrative contract were only a few years down the road, especially considering Bradley wasn't playing football anymore, resulting in a significant drop in income. Even in high school after a game where he had scored a couple of touchdowns, a few local businessmen would shake Bradley's hand following the game, and when the shake was over, there would be a crisp $100 bill left in his hand while at the same time the good ol' boys and rednecks would leave cans of beer or bottles of vodka in the front seat of his car.

Since Bradley didn't drink, Stacy would help take care of the liquor, and there was always more than she could drink. Stacy started hiding the excess bottles of liquor claiming she was "Saving for a raining day."

Since Bradley wouldn't drink with her and he didn't want her to drink on a daily basis, Stacy eventually became a closet drinker. She would only drink vodka, and like the old ads from Smirnoff would say, "Our Vodka will leave you breathless." That was good news for Stacy. She could drink vodka on the rocks all day and hide it from Bradley that same night.

As the months passed by the drinking increased. Finally Bradley moved into the guest bedroom, and the communication between the two of them became almost non-existent. Despite this Bradley needed someone to love him and, even though Stacy was more in love with the bottle than him, she was better than having no one. However, Bradley had often thought that if he could find someone to love him, he would leave Stacy in a heartbeat.

But now all the emotions with Stacy had to be pushed aside considering the newest troubled hand he had been dealt. He wasn't certain what he was going to say to Becky, Ricky's wife. Bradley had called Watkins Funeral Home in Lawrence and learned that the funeral was going to be on Saturday. Today was Thursday. The auto accident had occurred early Wednesday morning around 1:00am. He was going to the funeral mainly as a friend of both Ricky and Rebecca. After all he and Ricky had been teammates from fourth grade Pee Wee League all the way through their senior year in high school.

Bradley certainly remembered Becky. She was practically the only Stampede cheerleader who had made certain that he had not been in her panties. She had actually lived across the street and two houses down from him during school. She had been blessed with beautiful dark skin and an athletic build. As she was maturing, she was always riding a bicycle or jogging, absorbing the sun's abundant rays while wearing nylon soccer shorts and a tube top.

He remembered studying her legs, wishing that someday his legs were as muscular as Rebecca's. Even though her breasts had been small, he had stared at their contours in her tube tops, as he thought about his hand in a naturally-cupped position, fitting perfectly over one of them. Naturally he had often fantasized about having sex with Rebecca.

One summer evening, he had been alone with Rebecca. She had thrown a dance in her driveway on the weekend of July 4th. Rebecca and Bradley were juniors, and before the night was over, it seemed that every kid between the ninth and twelfth grade was in the neighborhood. About midnight, three cars loaded with football players from Malvern arrived to crash the party. The Panthers had always been a main rival of the Stampede.

The Stampede was known for traveling to surrounding communities to test out their skills on the willing co-eds. However, as protective as mother bears with their cubs, the Stampede also protected their own girls from outsiders.

The male classmates would comment that, "We may not want to service all of our women, but by God nobody else had better try while any of the Stampede were around."

That night during the street dance, several Malvern Panthers walked up and started looking around in an effort to assess the ladies and the situation. Within seconds there was a crowd of both Stampede football players and a group of guys who were just *cool* but not into organized sports. Bradley stood in front feeling like General Patton's Army was behind him.

It was a hot night, and Bradley had been dancing non-stop for several songs. Sweat soaked the sleeveless shirt he was wearing. With the lights from the corner streetlight shining on him and all the perspiration from dancing, his muscles appeared larger than they actually were. Bradley stood tall, flexed his triceps and said, "What a pleasure it is to have visitors in the neighborhood."

Turning and looking over his shoulder toward his troops, he smiled and commented, "Without their football pads on, the Panthers don't look very big, do they?"

Ricky Alexander replied loud enough for the Malvern players to hear, "Not big at all. I sure hope they don't let a few moments of bravery ruin them for the rest of their lives. Everyone knows that humiliation is something you just never get over."

"Okay dudes, here's the deal," Bradley instructed, "You can all just simply turn around, get back into that piece of shit automobile that brought you here, and haul your asses out of our neighborhood, and no one will get hurt or embarrassed."

"What if we're not in a hurry to leave?" asked the one with a panther tattooed on his arm.

Then it's simple," Bradley said with an ear-to-ear grin and voice loud enough for the action-hungry Stampede and the hell-raisers to hear. "I'm going to drag you – talking personally to the tattooed guy – over by that oak tree," pointing to a large oak in Becky's front yard, "then I'm going to give you a good ole'-fashioned ass whipping."

Then with a waving motion of his hand toward his comrades, Bradley continued, "While I'm teaching you some proper Lakeside Stampede manners, my friends are going to take your buddies out, one at a time for a quiet ride in the county and drop them off with nothing on but their shoes. When that's finished, we're going to flip your piece of shit car over on its side. Yes, this is going to be one hell of a night. Let's get this party started!"

"Hey Bradley, we didn't come here looking for any trouble, we were just looking for some fun," Tattoo said while holding both hands out in front of him with palms facing upward.

The music had been turned off. Even the frogs and crickets held out for Bradley's reply. "We are the ones who are going to have some fun if you don't get the hell out of Dodge, and I think now is a good time for you to scoot."

"Okay guys, let's hit the road. The numbers aren't quite in our favor." Tattoo took two steps, turned around and started walking toward the car. The rumble was over, and not a punch had been thrown.

Later that night, after the dance had ended and most had gone home, Bradley sat down on the back steps with Rebecca. He was waiting for the right moment to make his move when she said, "Bradley, I want to thank you for saving my party tonight. If a fight had started, I know the police would have come and broken up the dance making all of us go home. I look at you like the big brother I never had."

Bradley's desire, smoldering in his body, was quickly extinguished as if cold water had just been thrown on him. Bradley looked into her hazel eyes, regretfully kissed her on the forehead and said, "Any time, when you need a friend or a big brother, just look around; I'll be close."

He stood slowly, blew her a kiss and walked away. Rebecca watched him leave, wondering what she had done wrong. He stopped thinking about having sex with Rebecca from that moment on.

Then ringing of the cell phone startled Bradley out of his trance.

"Honey, where are you?" Stacy had a strong premonition that something was wrong. Bradley was usually extremely predictable, but these last couple of days had been an emotional roller coaster.

While looking out the window, trying to spot something familiar, searching for a mileage sign and not seeing anything, he took a shot at an answer. "I'm almost to Joplin and making pretty good time. I was just about to call," Bradley said as he passed a sign that said Butler, Missouri, 50 Miles. That meant he was about thirty miles passed Joplin. He was making better time than he thought. Thinking about high school days must have made his foot heavy.

"I'll stop by tomorrow and see Rebecca, and then I'll head home right after the funeral on Saturday. Stacy, I'm getting off the phone; I'll call you when I'm headed back to Hot Springs," Bradley pushed *end* on his cell phone and started drifting back to his old high school days again.

CHAPTER 16
SIGHT FOR SORE EYES

"May I help you?" asked the man in the three-piece dark navy suit.

Bradley inched slowly into the foyer of the Watkins Funeral Home. "Alexander?"

The three-piece suit kept direct eye contact with Bradley and nodded his head toward a hallway to the left. Bradley started down the hallway toward the room that held his high school friend, Ricky Alexander.

He noticed how quiet it was inside the funeral home, soft music in the background was the only thing audible. Looking around, he noticed that every Jesus on the wall was illuminated with its own spotlight. There was a box of tissue on every table beside every lamp. Although Bradley was new to the insurance business and had sold a couple of hundred life insurance policies, he had never had a death claim. The policy on Ricky was his first, and the primary beneficiary of the policy was Tony. Rebecca would not benefit from the policy at all. There hadn't been time to think about selling Ricky a policy that would have taken care of Rebecca upon his death. There hadn't even been time to send the application in to the home office, thus the application was still lying on Bradley's desk.

He inched toward and then peered into the chamber room. The casket was almost centered in the middle of the room, but nearer the back wall. The music was low and the lights were indirect, giving the room a dull, numbing feeling. Looking around he noticed the lack of visitors but an abundance of flowers. Spring had not arrived in Kansas same as it had in Arkansas, so the beautiful blooming flowers and plants brightened the day from the frigid outside temperature somewhere in the mid-thirties.

Then he noticed her ... standing up on her tiptoes, reaching to remove a card from a flower arrangement resting on a platform sticking out of the wall. Bradley had not seen her face, but he certainly remembered her legs. Those calf muscles could only belong to Rebecca.

Bradley, while remaining as quiet as possible, observed her. It has been several years since he had seen her, and even longer since he had talked to her.

Ricky and Rebecca exchanged their vows with the local Justice of the Peace, Bill McCracken, two weeks after graduation and then moved to Lawrence, Kansas the following week. Bradley faintly remembered that Ricky had big dreams about working on a cattle feed lot owned by Rebecca's cousin. Neither Ricky nor Rebecca attended college. She had always dreamed of a large family and a country-style house surrounded by a white fence, horses, and a pond jumping with catfish.

Bradley didn't know if either had accomplished any of their goals. He hadn't thought of of them until Tony had said that he and Ricky were in business together. She still had the figure of a cheerleader. In what Bradley would call a Sunday dress, Rebecca looked great. He had to remember that he wasn't picking her up to go to the prom. Her husband, his friend, has been killed in an auto accident. *Watch your manners, Tiger. After all, you're married yourself you know.*

He cleared his throat, and Rebecca turned to face the door. Their eyes met. She blinked as if seeing a mirage and unconsciously smoothed out her dress. A smile slowly expanded east to west until her grin couldn't stretch any further. Then north and south until her perfect white teeth warmed the entire room. She was a long way from the skinny neighbor with braces that Bradley had once remembered.

"Bradley Clevenger? Is that you?" Rebecca floated across the room to him and threw her arms around his neck. She held on as if she were drowning in the ocean and had just been saved by the lifeguard. Tears were streaming down her face when she finally eased her grip and looked into his eyes.

"What are you doing here?"

He could see her eyes brighten as her face suddenly became ten years younger.

"I can't believe it. I haven't seen you in years."

He smiled but said nothing as Rebecca took a deep breath and sighed with relief, "Thank you for being here; I feel so alone."

"I had to come, Rebecca." He touched her face. "Both you and Ricky mean a lot to me, and I couldn't believe it when I heard about Ricky's accident.

"Come sit with me." She led Bradley to an area with high-backed chairs and a coffee table. "Fill me in on what's happening in your life."

"Give me a few minutes alone with Ricky and then I'll be all yours."

Bradley approached the casket, noticing the beauty of the box that held his friend from years past. He had never seen a casket so colorful. A big sky scene completely engulfed the inside cover of the lid with mountains surrounding a field dotted with cattle grazing by a lake with weeping willows along one bank. On the other side of the lake was a levee raised eight to ten feet above the water level. An Appaloosa stallion stood looking over the lake with its head held high and its mane blowing in the wind. The reflection of the magnificent animal shimmered on the water. On the front side of the casket was a boy running down a dirt road pulling a kite behind him. The kite was barely off the ground with a big brown dog jumping in an effort to catch the tail in its jaws.

Both scenes carried a certain level of peace. The box, what was now Ricky's final home, was beautiful. Looking inside, Bradley recognized his friend. He was dressed in a dark blue, pin-striped suit and he had his hair slicked back Wall Street style. He looked peaceful.

Closing his eyes, Bradley spoke silently to Ricky. "I'm so sorry, my friend...that I didn't keep in touch with you after we graduated. I'm also sorry that I didn't write a life insurance policy on you that would've given Rebecca a way to pay off your house and whatever other bills you may have. I am glad that I was able to take care of Tony with the business policy on you. The proceeds from that life policy will allow Tony to find another partner, but it won't help the person who will need it most, Rebecca. I can't believe I even wrote those policies."

Bradley opened his tear-filled eyes and looked at Ricky. Bradley's eyes looked at every inch of Ricky's face, his smooth skin, the faint traces of make-up on his nose, and lipstick that Ricky would never have given approval to be worn. His chin was closely shaven…then, Bradley's inspection stopped upon Ricky's neck.

Bradley dabbed a tissue to dry his eyes. Looking back down, he focused on Ricky's neck again. The make-up couldn't cover the blue-black bruise on his upper throat at larynx level. There was also a bruise about six inches long on the left side of his neck. There were more traumas and bruising all around his neck than he had anticipated. It looked as though someone with vise grip hands had choked the life from Ricky, but only a couple of people knew that was exactly what had happened.

CHAPTER 17
BURN A LITTLE LESS HOT

Bradley joined Rebecca in a corner sitting area. She looked tired and lost. "Becky, I know this has been hard on you. I'm surprised that none of Ricky's family is here."

"Oh, they're here all right. They're driving me crazy! With eight of them in town, I don't believe I've had a moment to myself since this began. I've even got Ricky's aunt and uncle from Bismarck staying at my house. They were all here about an hour ago, talking about how he should be wearing something different and complaining about the songs I've picked out for the funeral. I told them this morning that they could change the music if they thought it would make Ricky burn a little less hot when he gets to Hell.

That comment put them in a frenzy of telling me how cold and cruel I am. Ricky's first cousin, Mary Margaret, even tossed her hair and said that I never gave him the affection he needed and deserved. I wondered at the time if maybe she had wanted a try at it."

Bradley could feel the hostility Rebecca felt toward the Alexander family. He crossed his legs, slumped down in the high-back chair, raised his eyebrows and with a *tell-me-more* expression he encouraged Rebecca to let it all out.

"They're probably huddled up in the parking lot right now trying to decide who is going to tell me that I'm in charge of paying for the funeral. I knew I couldn't count on them for any help." Rebecca pulled a couple of tissues out of the holder located on the table. Her eyes were overflowing as she shook her head in anguish saying, "I don't know where I'll be in thirty days. The funeral will eat up our savings. The funeral guy said it would cost no less than $15,000. Honestly, I wouldn't have the money if it was $150. We owe money on two cars, furniture and several other things. I may have to put this funeral on a credit card. The Alexander's think we had a lot of money, but we didn't. I'm sorry to be pouring my guts out to you, but I haven't had anyone to talk to other than my in-laws ever since Ricky's death. I don't dare talk money to them. They think I'm the one who always wanted to drive a new car or go on a big vacation each year. It wasn't me who spent money like it grew on trees. Ricky was the one who tried to impress the neighbors with his ability to make money."

Rebecca was getting angry again. Her eyes were flashing around the room as she leaned forward toward Bradley, and with a deep breath continued, "But we weren't getting ahead, we were falling farther and farther behind. Every time the sun came up Ricky was spending money, and when the sun set we were deeper in debt." Rebecca's mood had slowly changed from sadness and sentimentality to anger and resentfulness for having been used and abused.

"Bradley, I've never told anyone this, but Ricky had a gambling problem. I don't know if you've ever thought of the cattle business as legalized gambling, but that's what it was to Ricky. He would buy cattle one day and sell them the next without ever having laid eyes on them. He would gamble day-to-day on the price of cattle. Sometimes he would make money, but sometimes not. He was always gambling that the cost of feed would not rise or the rain would come at the right time. Ricky would either make or lose thousands of dollars each day. He would brag about the times he'd make money, but I could tell by his reactions the days when he had been wrong with his predictions and had lost money. He wouldn't talk to me, and he drank and smoked even more."

Rebecca finally caught her breath and looked at Bradley with moist eyes, "You drove all this way here to say goodbye to one of your friends, and I'm saying things that you probably don't want to hear much less even know about. I'm sorry Bradley."

"It's fine Rebecca. I'm also here because of you. I want to do whatever I can to help you through this tragic time in your life."

Rebecca looked at Bradley with a perplexed look on her face and said, "Tragic? I've not thought of that particular word in reference to Ricky's death. Relieved is the word I've associated with from the moment the police came to my home and told me about the so-called accident."

She said the words *so-called* with a tone of sarcasm that froze the room, even making the stereo take a break from the easy-listening, religious tape that had been paying.

"Rebecca, you're not suggesting that the car wreck was anything other than an accident?" Bradley sat up straight and leaned slightly forward in his chair looking for whatever reaction Rebecca might show.

"I don't know what I'm thinking or saying, Bradley. I do know that I feel a weight has been lifted off of my shoulders with Ricky gone. I know he can't get us in debt any farther than we are now. I can handle the legal bills such as credit cards, cars, and such. I don't know what will happen to the illegal debts that Ricky has piled up. I can tell you one thing for certain – Tony LaTour is going to be mad as hell that he didn't collect from Ricky before the accident."

Bradley couldn't help staring at Rebecca wondering if he had heard the name correctly.

CHAPTER 18
A PROMISE IS A PROMISE

Granny's Kitchen had always been a local favorite for a plate lunch and a bowl of blackberry cobbler. Every inch of wall space was covered with a picture or a sign showing Hot Springs as it was a generation ago. The tablecloths were red and white checkerboard patterned, and the flatware was in a metal bucket placed in the center of each table. A twine-bottomed rocking chair stood court at the head of each table.

Granny's Kitchen Diner attracted both locals and tourists, as it had been in business for over seventy years. Tables were almost always filled with families or visitors who were either laughing or swapping events of the day, and generally acting as if there wasn't a problem or worry to be had. All tables at least appeared that way except for the one next to the wall in the very back of the café, because it was there Jim Boy and Tony sat.

Jim Boy was smoking a Cuban cigar. The way he held his cigar in his hand with his pinky finger sticking out showed off a one karat diamond ring. He wore a double-breasted suit complete with alligator shoes, and his tie matched the silk scarf peeking out of his suit's breast pocket. Jim Boy looked as if he could have appeared on next month's *Gentlemen's Quarterly* or *Cigar Aficionado*. He was drinking a black label Bush Mills and water.

Tony was smoking a cigarette while drinking black coffee. When one cigarette started burning into the filter, Tony would simply light the next one from the end of the smoldering cotton. The smell of tar-soaked cotton lingered in the air around them. Tony's hair was slicked back and looked dirty, his clothes were a mess, looking as if he had slept in them, and the red in his eyes was overlooked only due to the constant jerking of his head to see if someone were walking up behind him.

"Tony, don't be so fucking nervous. Calm down! This is a public restaurant, and you're drawing attention to us. Your debt of $200,000 is not due today. According to my calculation you still have approximately forty-eight to seventy-two hours left before you need to start watching your back."

"Jim Boy," Tony was trying to light another cigarette with his hands shaking, "I had nothing to do with Freeway's getting the stuff stolen. I need more time."

Tony dropped his coffee cup when the waitress walked up behind him and placed her hand on his shoulder. The coffee splashed on the table speckling the front of Jim Boy's shirt, tie and suit coat. However, Jim Boy never flinched. His cold stare penetrated all the way to the back of Tony's brain.

"I'm sorry honey. It looked as if you were trying to shed your skin by jumping so high," the waitress commented as she started sopping up the spilled coffee. "Can I get you another cup?"

"No thanks, but I do need a pack of those Rolaids that you keep up by the cash register." Tony had beads of perspiration on his forehead. His right foot was on its toes with the heel two or three inches off the floor tapping uncontrollably at what seemed to be ninety miles per hour.

"I need about two more weeks, and then I'll come up with the cash one way or another." Tony's voice was low but his eyes were begging. "I've got an ace in the hole that I think will bring me your money and more." Tony was thinking about the recording he had of Bradley's boasting ...

"When I say you are covered, you are covered!"

If Bradley didn't come through with the money on Alexander's life insurance policy, then blackmail was the next step. A call to the Insurance Department and an Error and Omission Lawsuit filed against him could cost Bradley his insurance agency. In a court of law, Bradley would be caught in the middle where a common man goes up against a huge insurance company.

***

The testimony could go something like this:

Judge: "Bradley, is it true that you met with Ricky Alexander and Tony LaTour at your office to discuss life insurance to cover their business?"

Bradley: (looking nervous because he realizes that to admit that Alexander was not present would cost him his license) "Yes your Honor."

Judge: "When you were talking to both Alexander and LaTour, did you give them the impression that as soon as they signed the application they would be covered?"

Bradley glances over to Tony and makes eye contact.

Tony gives Bradley a smile and thinks, "Make a decision my old friend. If you say *yes* then you'll be reprimanded, but I'll receive $600,000 from that fine company of yours. Say *no* and I will tell the judge that Ricky Alexander wasn't present at all, and that I had signed Ricky's name to the application because you had instructed me to do so. Then for good measure, I'll play the tape that says, *when I say you're covered, you're covered!* Then you'll lose your license and become a landscaper that specializes in lawn mowing while I – being innocent – will still receive the promised $600,000."

***

"Hey!" Jim Boy barked as he reached across the table and gently slapped Tony's face in an effort to bring him back to reality. "Don't fade out on me while I'm discussing business with you. Today's a great day for two reasons ... because you're alive and because I think you're a man of your word. You are a LaTour, and so far the LaTour's have been trustworthy. I'm actually going to grant you more time."

Jim Boy took another sip of his Bush Mills as Tony whimpered, "You'll never regret this, Jim Boy."

"Shut the fuck up! You've said all you're entitled to say tonight," then leaning in Jim Boy continued, "Now listen to me, and then get the hell out of my face and go get me my money."

Jim Boy lowered his voice and with squinted eyes went on to state further, "I'm not telling you how much additional time I'm giving you. Your father, Johnny, is still running the bookmaking business in town for some of my friends. I hear he's doing a good job. If I let my friends know that a LaTour, the son of their employee, has fucking cheated me out of $200,000 fucking dollars, then they will assume that it must be some sort of an inherited problem. You know what I'm talking about, a fucking genetic thing. They may even think your old man could be skimming a little off the top to help his fucking little boy out of trouble. As we sometimes say, if you're going to kill za snake, you have to cut off the snake's head. Your papa is still the head of your family. Get me my fucking money before you wake up some morning with your papa's head looking down at you from the top of your bedpost."

Tony felt a rush down his spine and his words stuck in his throat while he was trying to think of something worth saying. The sweat started running down his cheeks, dripping onto the red and white checkerboard tablecloth.

Then Jim Boy closed the meeting by saying, "NOW GET THE FUCK OUT OF HERE!"

CHAPTER 19
NO EVIDENCE

Bradley glanced around the church, still surprised at the small number of attendees gathered to say their goodbyes to Ricky Alexander. At the last moment, Rebecca decided to have Ricky's body cremated. She told the Alexander family that it had always been a request of Ricky's. He wanted a viewing of his body for a day or two so the family could have their final time with him and have closure on the event. Then after everyone who wanted to see him had paid their last respects, Ricky had asked to be cremated and his ashes given to his mother.

Rebecca was quite believable in her fabricated story, and even squeezed out a tear or two as she told Ricky's mother his final wishes.

There were several reasons for the cremation. One was the cost. Rebecca had told the funeral director she was out of money and couldn't pay. Behind closed doors she had told the three piece suit, "Pull that bastard out of that Barnham and Bailey coffin, spray paint it black, and sell it to some other fool."

The cremation was about 10% of what the casket alone was going to cost. On the other hand, giving Ricky's ashes to his mother – what a joy! Rebecca could wash her hands of the Alexander family once and for all. She laughed to herself when she was telling MawMaw Alexander, "Please take good care of him," while she was thinking, I hope he doesn't end up in your vacuum cleaner or worse the cat doesn't use him for a litter box, even though that's probably what he deserves. The final reason for the cremation was the one that convinced her to have it completed quickly.

"Becky, there's something else I need to tell you. I believe Ricky was a mafia hit due to the fact that he owed a lot of money to a man named Jim Boy back in Hot Springs."

Becky raised her eyebrows, "Am I in danger?"

"I don't know. What I do know is there was a life insurance

policy taken out on Ricky with Tony being the primary beneficiary or the person that gets the money."

"Tell me more."

"I'm somewhat involved, because I was the agent that wrote the policy. I lied on the application saying that I had witnessed Ricky signing. Of course I hadn't, and I feel like my insurance license is in jeopardy, not to mention that I also think my life is in limbo. If the police think this is a murder, they will have an autopsy and all kind of shit will hit the fan."

The investigators from the Premier Insurance Company would want to check into possible foul play starting with digging into their finances. If it was ever discovered Ricky had been running a debt with illegal activities, she could be in danger as well.

After a long discussion with Bradley, cremation was a quick solution to all evidence of the accident. The cremation was less money and MawMaw Alexander could drive away with Ricky buckled into the front passenger seat.

CHAPTER 20
WORKING TOGETHER HARMONIOUSLY

Rebecca was looking out from the bay window into the back yard when the phone rang,

"Rebecca its Bradley, are you doing okay?"

"Sure. I'm just sitting here wondering if I should pack up, load a U-Haul and get going, or simply walk away and leave it all behind. By the way ... where are you? I looked for you after the service yesterday, but you were gone."

There was silence on the other side of the phone.

"I'm still here in Lawrence. I need to talk to you, but I wanted to make sure the Alexander's had left town first. Right now I'm downtown at the Mass Street Deli."

"They're gone, and you sure missed a show. The three piece suit walked over and picked up Ricky just as the last of the marching-out song was being played, and then put him in the vault behind the counter in the business office. When Maw Maw Alexander asked for his ashes, the suit said not until someone paid him the $1,500 owed for the cremation and services. They were both standing taller than normal and staring at each other when I decided it was as good a time as any to turn and take my mourning self out of there and head for somewhere else."

"Jesus, I wish I had been a fly on the ceiling. Any idea how it ended?"

"I called back a few hours later to hear what had happened. The suit told me that a cousin who had ridden in the same car with Ricky's parents ended up putting the fifteen hundred on a Visa card, plus he bought a bus ticket back home. He said he wasn't about to ride in the same car with a dead person, even if that person would fit into a one-pound coffee can. I wish I could have seen it with my own eyes."

"Bradley, you said you needed to talk to me?" Rebecca looked around to see if the room needed a quick pick-up.

"I know it sounds weird, but I'll take a cab over to your house at about dark. Leave the door unlocked because I want to get inside from the street as quickly as possible."

***

"Where the hell is he? His answering machine is full, his office is closed, no one knows where he is and I'm running out of time."

Tony paced the floor. It had been a couple of days since he had talked to Jim Boy and the stress was building again. Tony had a game plan in his head, and it was foolproof. With Ricky dead and Tony the primary beneficiary of the life insurance policy worth $600,000 his plan would take care of everyone's needs. Jim Boy would get his $200,000 grand, and Tony would ride off into the sunset with a hard-earned $400,000. The plan was sure to work if Tony could get to Bradley and make certain that the claim on Ricky was being handled. Tony needed to get the money from the Premier Insurance Company before Jim Boy said the clock's time had run out. Sounds simple enough, but Tony's blood pressure foretold another outcome.

Bradley's decision-making process was blown all to hell. He knew what he wanted to do and how to pull it off, but he also knew that if he made a mistake it would cost him his life. Bradley felt short of breath as he waited for the phone to start ringing.

When the phone did finally ring, Bradley jumped as if electricity were running through him. After the first ring, he was breathing deeply after noticing the caller ID noted a *private caller*. He carefully picked up the phone, said hello, and was immediately answered with a silence accompanied by slow, heavy breathing.

"Jim Boy, this is Bradley Clevenger with the Premier Insurance Company. I realize that you don't know me, but I have information that my conscience won't allow me to keep confidential any longer."

Bradley was talking into the phone with no feedback whatsoever from the other end. His mind stretched to the limit. Tony was within days of going to the insurance commissioner to report a misrepresentation. If the insurance department needed some press or someone to butcher, then Bradley's career could become history within weeks.

Tony would tell the commissioner that Bradley had sold him a life insurance policy guaranteed by his agency. Although Tony had purchased the policy with criminal intentions in mind, that was beside the point, as Tony would never admit to any wrongdoing. The agent, Bradley, had accepted the premium and looked away when Tony signed Ricky's name on the dotted line. He was seeing his career come to an end ... a football player with a blown knee and now an insurance agent found guilty of a claim of misrepresentation might as well catch the next train out of town. That kind of claim is the same as a malpractice in the medical profession. It's the kiss of death to a career.

Jim Boy broke the silence with, "Why should I meet with you?"

"I'm an insurance agent, and one of my clients is Tony LaTour," Bradley quickly looked behind him feeling guilty and fearing that someone was watching him. "I think I should inform you of something that I believe is intended to happen to you."

"What are you saying Mr. Insurance Man? Are you saying that my life is in danger? Tell me something that I don't know. My life has been in danger ever since I made the decision to make my living from the streets. You had better tell me something I don't know before I decide to end this phone call."

It's not your life that's in danger, but rather one of your investments." Bradley could hear the silence return to the earpiece, as he definitely had Jim Boy's attention now. "I believe I have some information for you that would be of great interest."

"Okay, let's meet at Granny's Kitchen downtown. I'll be there at 9:00am sitting at a table along the back wall."

"I'm sorry Jim Boy, but I'm out of state and won't be back in Hot Springs until tomorrow night. How about 10:00pm at Granny's Kitchen?"

"I'm there; make certain you are." The phone went silent.

***

Jerry Carter, the District Manager with Premier Insurance Company, was about to pull his hair out, and at this stage of his career he only had a comb-over left at best.

"Where the hell is Bradley? He calls me to inform the company of a death claim, and now we can't find him anywhere." Jerry paced his office while occasionally glancing out of the window of his training center fruitlessly hoping to see Bradley pulling into the parking lot any minute. Bradley knows he should be in constant contact with me to make certain that this death claim is properly handled. The company needs to be notified, and someone needs to call the family and let them know about the policy, not to mention he is making an old man out of me.

"New agents! Shit, it's worse than teaching grade school. They think they know everything when most of the time all they do is fuck things up!" Jerry was now looking for his bottle of Mylanta. "I tell them the same damn thing over and over again, and now I've come to believe it goes in one ear and out the other." Jerry collapsed into his high-backed executive chair, ran his hand through his hair making one side about four inches longer than the other side and thought about a cabin on Lake Hamilton. "I need to get out of this business."

***

When Bradley arrived at Rebecca's house, he noticed the table set for two. There was a wine bottle in a bucket of ice on the cabinet next to several sacks of Chinese food from the Magic Wok. Rebecca was sitting in the family room. There was no TV on or music. She was just sitting there alone quietly thinking while sipping on a glass of plum wine.

Rebecca had not heard from the Alexander family since they left town. Maw Maw had been driving while Ricky was buckled safely in the front seat with pillows cushioning his sides.

It had been good seeing Bradley again. She had gone years without thinking about him. Bradley was the stud, the one every girl had dreamed about while wanting his head to turn their way. Rebecca had counted herself out of the running as a small kid. She would watch the other girls flirt and throw themselves at Bradley. They couldn't care less if it was for one night or a lifetime. Actually the rumor had been that one night was a lifetime. Rebecca had never wanted to get into that rat race. Her self-esteem had been far too low, so she didn't think she had deserved someone like Bradley.

Now Ricky was a different story. He was popular, but he had always felt as though he was getting shafted by someone. In sports

Ricky thought the coaches weren't giving him enough time to show what he could do, but basketball was his real love. He had the expandable pole and backboard in his driveway at home. With the goal dropped down to the height of nine feet, Ricky could dazzle the neighborhood kids with spectacular dunks typically only seen in the NBA. Often he was seen running out Highway 270 East towards Malvern during the heat of the day, and if it was daylight, Ricky was working out. However, if it was nighttime he was drinking or gambling.

The coaches knew both sides of Ricky. For instance, he was a born choker. During crucial moments toward the end of a game Ricky had always wanted the ball, wanted the last shot and wanted to be the game winner. Unfortunately, he could never find the hole. He would either hit a rim shot or bounce it off the backboard too hard. Either way, he simply could not get a ball to fall through the hoop during the last minute of the game. Sometimes, you would swear there had to be a piece of glass covering the hoop. *No one* could ever remember Ricky winning the game with a last second shot. If the goal had been set at nine feet, Ricky could have driven the lane and started his cruise around the free throw line with the ball palmed high over his head as if pleading for any fool to try to stop him, then he would have slammed the ball through the bottom of the net. However, at ten feet his best bet was a finger roll toward the rim that would eventually circle the rim a couple of times before finally dropping to the floor to the groans and moans of the crowd as they watched another close game slip away. For his tradition of losing games, the coaches decided to use him only in the first and third quarters, while using Bradley during the last ten seconds of the game for a one-on-one show that ended most of the time with Bradley elbow-deep in the net to the sound of the buzzer signaling the end of the game.

Rebecca had wasted her best years with Ricky. She was always thinking and wishing that things were different. The stress of the cattle business combined with wondering if they would have enough money to pay the next month's bills was a constant topic, and if the money situation wasn't enough of a problem, her sex life was even worse. When he was happy and sober, his plumbing worked, but drunk and depressed he couldn't get it up. Most nights Rebecca went to to bed alone and fell asleep thinking about why she hadn't dumped Ricky before they ever got married. She would have been better off marrying one of the Warren boys who were in line to inherit their father's mobile home business.

But today Rebecca was thinking about Bradley. He had come to her rescue as a knight in shining armor. When she needed a friend more than anything in the world, Bradley was there to comfort her. He tied up the loose ends surrounding Ricky's questionable death and gave her the strength to deal with the Alexander's. Rebecca was now trying to deal with what the present and future might have in store for her. The house was mostly quiet now. The phone didn't ring, and the grass in the yard was growing up around the McGrew Real Estate sign that had gone up the day after Ricky's death stating *For Sale.*

CHAPTER 21
SLEIGHT OF HAND

B radley parked in the alley behind Granny's Kitchen, next to the Chrysler PT Cruiser that belonged to Jim Boy. As Bradley stepped out of the car and hit the lock button on his hand-held remote, a shadow walked up beside him.

"Mr. Clevenger," the shadow spoke, "I need to search you for wires and hardware."

Bradley jumped and stumbled back onto his car. "Shit! Man you scared the hell out of me."

Bradley carried with him a file folder that contained a new application, two changes of beneficiary forms, a latex glove and a black pen. The pen was the same one used when Tony completed the paperwork for the policy on Ricky Alexander.

Bradley was selling, and he hoped that Jim Boy was buying.

"Remove your jacket and put your hands on top of the car," No-Neck said, while holding a hand wand that detected any sound waves, whether sending or receiving. As he moved the wand slowly over every inch of Bradley, a smile came to No-Neck's face. He shook his head side-to-side and commented, "Bradley Clevenger! I used to watch you every Friday night. I still remember the Lake Hamilton game when the Stampede was a seven point underdog and the winner of the game would qualify for the state playoffs. You ran through them like flour though a sifter. You scored three touchdowns and we won 28 -12 in front of about five thousand of Hot Springs' finest. Wow! What a night." No-Neck had temporarily forgotten what his duties were for the evening while becoming a fan again.

"It's sure good to see you Bradley and I want to thank you for some great years on the football field. I made a lot of money betting on you and the Stampede during those years."

He lowered his voice and in a whisper, said, "Do whatever Jim

Boy says you should do. He's in a bloody mood, and I don't want you to end up like some of the others."

Bradley looked at him and replied, "Thanks." It had a strange feeling saying thanks to someone who doesn't want Bradley to be the next victim.

No-Neck clicked on a walkie-talkie and said, "He's clean boss and on his way in."

Bradley noticed the restaurant was empty – not only empty of customers – but also of workers. The lighting inside was low at best. Jim Boy had met an hour earlier with the manager and offered enough cash money to get the restaurant to close early and send the entire staff of workers home. No-Neck led Bradley to the only illuminated table where Jim Boy sat alone, back against the wall with his Cuban cigar smoldering.

Bradley slowed down to an almost dead stop and watched Jim Boy as he edged closer while Jim Boy did the same. Without moving a muscle, they locked eyes. There was no friendly gesture or smile, only a cold stare as Bradley reached the table and stood at attention in front of Jim Boy, awaiting his instructions before making his next move. Bradley instinctively knew he was on Jim Boy's turf and he was going to show respect.

"Please, sit down, Mr. Clevenger.

Bradley put the folder on the table and slowly lowered himself into the chair.

"Mr. Clevenger, I believe you said something about one of my investments being on shaky ground. Why don't you fill me in on what you know, and why I should be meeting with you tonight?"

"I have a client who wants you dead."

"I understand that you are in the insurance business, and I suspect there may be several individuals who feel that way. But I don't follow what you and I have in common with someone wanting to see harm come my way."

"Several weeks ago, Tony LaTour came into my office. He told me of a business relationship between the two of you. He didn't go into any details about your business arrangement, but he purchased four life insurance policies: one on himself for six hundred thousand dollars with Ricky being the beneficiary and another on Ricky for the same amount with himself being the beneficiary. He also purchased a third policy on Tony with you being the primary beneficiary and a policy on you with Tony being the primary beneficiary. Those last two policies were for a million bucks."

"Give me a short lesson Mr. Insurance Man. What does that mean?" Jim boy was tuned in as the veins in his neck and forehead started to swell.

"That last policy would pay you one million dollars upon the death of Tony. It would come to you tax free with no questions asked."

"Well, that would be very generous of my dear friend, but why would he buy a policy like that? What would be in it for Tony?"

"Well that's where it gets interesting. We also did paperwork on a policy with you being the insured, and upon your death the same amount of one million dollars would go to Tony."

Jim Boy took off his slightly tinted glasses and squinted at Bradley, "How could he do that without my knowing about it or giving permission?"

"I gave him the application to take with him, because he said he would be seeing you the next day, and he would get your signature at that time. I met with him the following evening, and he brought it back to me signed and ready to be sent to the company. I have it with me."

"So, what you're telling me is that you believe I'm a *dead man walking*?"

"What I'm telling you is I believe Tony thinks he will receive a million dollar check from my company if you stop breathing."

In that moment, both men were thinking more than they were talking. It seemed as if time was standing still between one man having finished a sentence while waiting on the other to provide an answer.

"Why haven't you sent the application in to your company?"

"I'm worried about my career. I've sent up a red flag recently, and now I'm trying to prevent another problem – namely fraud – that would end up drawing more unwanted attention to me."

"I'm confused, Mr. Insurance man. Maybe you'd better start from the beginning."

"A couple of weeks ago, I met with Tony LaTour in my office. I needed a big sale, and the commission that would come from it. You see I was trying to win a promotion. I thought I was doing a great job of selling, but it's now starting to look like I was being sold a bill of goods."

"Tony wanted life insurance policies. He took out a policy covering an old high school friend of ours, Ricky Alexander. The very next night Ricky was involved in a single-car accident and died from a broken neck. I hadn't even mailed the application into the company. It was still on my desk. I've now sent it on to the company, and I believe that Tony will receive a check for $600,000 within a week."

"Well that will heal several of LaTour's problems. I'm certain he's checking the mail every day." Jim Boy was starting to fidget as he was growing tired of the small talk.

"Not only is he checking the mail, but he's calling me several times a day. The one question he has asked several times is this, "If something happened to Jim Boy, would his check get processed just as smoothly as Ricky's?"

"I made a mistake of letting Tony sign Ricky's name on the application, and now I believe Tony had something to do with Ricky's accident. I can't say anything about it, because Tony knows I will lose my insurance license if the company finds out that I lied about the signatures."

Jim Boy's face was changing colors. With his hands clasped and his elbows on the table, his eyes centered on Bradley as he asked, "Do you think Tony is going to have me killed?"

"I do," Bradley stated; then he uttered a sigh of relief. "I haven't sent in the application, because I know if something happened to you with a policy of one million dollars, the investigators would come asking me all sorts of questions, and I would end up losing my career. Also, there's a lot of money changing hands, and none of it is crossing my palms. I'm a straight agent, loyal to my company and profession. I never wanted to get involved in what I think might be happening. I only wanted to win a trip. I don't want to get involved with your business or you, and now I don't ever want to see Tony again."

Bradley was getting short of breath, and his nerves were starting to unravel. "I know I will see him at least one more time, and that's when I deliver the check to him because Ricky is now dead."

"Your meeting with me tonight was risky." Jim Boy kept eye contact with Bradley as he unclasped his hands and slowly slid his right hand under the table and into his pocket. Bradley's heart fluttered while a wave of panic crossed his face. He froze as he watched Jim Boy's hand carefully come from under the table. Bradley was looking for a pistol, but instead it was a wad of money. Jim Boy peeled off five one hundred dollar bills and put them in front of Bradley.

"Bradley, this is for the info you have given me tonight. Also, I'm telling you that you are in no danger from me or any of my friends."

"Thank you, Jim Boy. I want no trouble with you. I only want to get this behind me so that I can resume my insurance career."

"Do you have anything else you need to say, or does this wrap it up?"

"That's it for me."

Then with a snap of Jim Boy's fingers, No-Neck who had been so glad to see Bradley appeared at the table and said, "Mr. Clevenger, I will walk you to your car now."

CHAPTER 22
SERVED WITH A SIDE OF NATIVE

Bradley was back at his office. On his desk lay a week's worth of unopened mail from the Premier Insurance Company. In his daily mail were usually news bulletins explaining a new product or procedure. Sometimes there was a report on what the competition was doing. It had now been a couple of weeks since Tony had sat across the desk thinking he was steering Bradley in the direction of completing a life insurance application on Ricky while Bradley, at the same time, felt that he was a super salesperson about to win a trip to paradise.

After checking out the brochure's pictures of deeply tanned, beautiful models and natives, Bradley had decided to go on the trip alone. Being alone would make it easy to slip away from the group of agents and spouses to find a different form of paradise, even if he had to pay for the affection. In one picture, a man lounged in a hammock with a topless native. She handed him a multi-colored drink, different shades of orange, topped off with a cocktail umbrella. Looking closely at the man in the hammock, a grin slowly crossed Bradley's face as he noticed the uncanny resemblance to himself.

CHAPTER 23
DADDY'S KNOW

Tony's father had hung around the track his entire life. Prior to becoming a pawn of the chosen pari-mutuel beneficiaries, Papa LaTour had worked as a stable boy while still in elementary school. He learned the ropes of working with horses, and spent as much time as possible at the stable.

"It's hard to stay away from a place that's as comfortable as your home." Papa LaTour was leaning on the top board of the gate that kept the mare, Abby Gail, in her stable. His right cowboy boot rested on the bottom rung of the gate. He had followed Abby Gail's career for several years. She had always been a consistent moneymaker by finishing in one of the top three spots in over 50 percent of her starts. She was a gentle mare, red with white stockings and a star on her forehead. Abby Gail was well known around the stables as having an *Aunt Bea* attitude, requiring very little attention.

Papa had his usual bunch of carrots and sugar cubes in his pocket when he arrived at Oaklawn. Several of the regulars at the stables would snort and get excited as soon as Papa came into view, instantly alerting the others there that the snack man was making his rounds.

"Abby Gail, I can't give you any carrots today because you're running this afternoon."

Abby Gail's upper lip flapped as she exhaled a sigh of disgust, appearing to understand totally what Papa had just stated.

"If you win, I'll stop by tomorrow for a victory celebration." Her large brown eyes bulged, and her head jerked back and forth, shaking her approval.

Papa usually stopped by each morning to walk through the stables, check on his favorite horses, visit with the trainers and pick up any tips that might be floating around. Knowing which horse was running to win and which was running to only position themselves for a later race was another key to making money at the track. This kind of knowledge made the betting child's play. It was clear that today Abby Gail was running to win.

Papa knew she should win, but the day had begun a little out of balance. His alarm clock failed to go off this morning, so his regular routine was running about thirty minutes late. He had set all of this aside and before leaving the house had removed the painting of Seattle Slew from the wall in the dining room. Behind the painting was a safe where Papa kept a stash of money he used for betting on sure things, and on this day he was going to bet it all on Abby Gail.

"Hey Pop, what's up?" Tony strolled up to Abby Gail's stall where Johnny LaTour was leaning up against the gate.

Johnny didn't turn around or even move to acknowledge Tony in any form or fashion as he leaned up against the gate next to his father and admired Abby Gail. All movement and sounds stopped for two or three minutes.

"What kind of shit do you have yourself in this time, Son?"

"I've got it all worked out, Pop. I'm letting it all fall into place, and then I'm going to be set for a long time. I'm even thinking about heading up north when this is all over. Maybe Chicago."

"Son, when was the last time you went to confession?" Papa LaTour still had not looked at Tony, but instead stared at the ground a few feet inside the stall.

"It's been a while Pop. Why do you ask?"

"Your mother and I tried to raise you to love the church. Father Boren talked to me a couple of Sundays ago. He said he hadn't seen you in several months, and that the confessions he hears can't be repeated to anyone – not even the law – and that he has a bad feeling about you. He's afraid that you might be mixed up in the shooting out by the Gorge where Freeway was killed. Drugs were involved, and he says you may be next."

Tony shuffled his feet nervously while his Papa still hadn't moved a muscle to even look at his son.

"I can't help you, Son. We are all responsible for our own actions, but promise me you'll go to confession soon. I met with Father Boren a couple days ago and received a blessing. I'm prepared to meet the Lord. I just don't want to meet him today. If something happened to you, I would sleep better knowing you had your affairs in order."

"Don't worry about me, Pop. I promise this thing is just about over. I wanted to stop by to tell you I love you."

Tony turned toward his dad, put both hands along the sides of his head, and kissed him on top of his head.

Papa LaTour's eyes slowly traveled up the lean body of Tony until they stared into the souls of one another. Papa had tears swelling while deep down he somehow knew he would never see his son again.

CHAPTER 24
BEHIND THE STABLE DOOR

The LaTour family started to draw together in the Eastgate neighborhood. The small Hot Springs airport buzzed with private aircraft coming in from Chicago, Kansas City, and Miami. It had been several years since the family had all gathered together. The last occasion had been the wedding of Naomi LaTour of Hot Springs to John Gravino from Chicago. Naomi and John had met as children, and it was expected that they would one day wed. During their June wedding, which had been held out at Garvan Gardens just outside of Hot Springs, the couple once stood on top of the arched bridge crossing the stream that flowed through the park.

But this was different, because this event was not a happy one. Papa LaTour had experienced a horrible death, which had been classified as an accident, but behind closed doors there was talk about who and why the hit had been called on Papa. Most mob executions are never investigated. The *Sentinel Record*, Hot Springs' daily newspaper, ran the news of Papa LaTour's death in the sports section. A new ride at Magic Springs Amusement Park commandeered the front page complete with color photos, but a murder at Oaklawn Park would be pushed into an obscure corner, hopefully never to be seen by any tourists, but it didn't take long for the rumors to start circulating.

The stable door had been locked from the outside, preventing Papa LaTour from escaping his death chamber. Abby Gail's hooves had been equipped with shoes that had razor sharp edges that would slash and slice with every contact. The inside of her stall had been completely destroyed. The wooden rails and walls were now splintered and broken. The floor of the stable appeared to be covered with redwood mulch due to the combination of pine wood and LaTour's blood. Abby Gail was also found dead. The autopsy revealed that her heart had exploded from a lethal dose of stimulants. The drugs caused Abby Gail's heart to beat faster and stronger. First, she would have become anxious, and then agitated, followed by an uncontrollable fury that had led to her destroying anything or anyone within reach. Her heart finally exploded, causing the lather-drenched, two thousand pound animal to drop beside the remains of Papa LaTour. As the blood ran from the nose and mouth of Abby Gail and mingled with the blood and brain mixture of her once longtime best friend, someone walked by the stable door, and with a gloved hand, slid the metal pin out of the hasp that had prevented Papa LaTour from fleeing.

CHAPTER 25
SIGNED, SEALED, DELIVERED

"Hello, this is Bradley."

"Hey, it's Tony. Did I catch you at a good time?"

"I'm in my car but what's on your mind other than do I have your check?"

"That's the only question that I need answered, Mr. Insurance Man."

"Tony, I don't have your check today, but I have talked to the claims department, and they said it would go out tomorrow by Federal Express. They usually make their deliveries to my office just before noon, so why don't you stop by around 1:00pm. I should be able to give you the check for Ricky's policy and get your signature, proving that you received the check. Then our business relationship will have to come to an end."

"It's been a pleasure doing business with you, Mr. Insurance man, and maybe we can do some future policies. You know that you are quite the salesperson, and I just can't say no to you." Tony laughed as he made that last comment.

"Tony, I'm not asking you any questions about the life policies, Ricky's death or your involvement in his death, because I know the answers. After you get your check, I never want to see or hear from you again. You can spend your money any way you want, but you will never get another dime from the Premier Insurance Company."

"Don't be a bad sport, my friend. We both got what we wanted out of this transaction. I'm getting loads of money and you won the sales promotion that will get you a plaque and a trip. I would think you would be tanning and packing your travel bag."

"Fuck you, Tony! You screwed me and my company, plus one of our high school friends is dead, and you will rot in Hell for your actions."

"As always, it's been great talking with you Bradley, and I'll see you tomorrow at 1:00pm at your office." The phone connection dropped, and Bradley started scrolling through his directory looking for Jim boy's phone number.

***

The Pier House is located at the end of Duval Street in Key West, Florida. Looking out West from the top floor where the penthouse is located is the Gulf of Mexico. Each day at sunset, the pier was the gathering place for all in Key West to watch the sun drop and disappear into the horizon. Many thought the main attraction was the sun, but looking around, street vendors and people of all types, sizes, colors and occupations could be seen from all angles. Some of them were selling music CDs and tie-dyed shirts reminiscent of a Grateful Dead or Phish concert.

Rebecca had been there about three hours when the spectacle began gathering steam.

Bradley had given her a one-way plane ticket and instructions to check into the Pier House and wait for additional instructions. When she checked into her room, there was an envelope with five one-hundred dollar bills. Laid out on the bed was a pair of blue jean shorts with frayed hems, flip flops, and a tie-dyed tank top. There was also a note instructing her to change clothes, and then go out onto the pier to watch the sun set. The message ended with a simple sentiment ... He she would hear from him in a couple days.

***

The door suddenly opened, and Tony stepped into Bradley's office.

"It's 1:00pm, and I'm right on time," Tony announced with an ear-to-ear, toothy grin. Walking into the office, he stepped over toward the couch and looked at the framed certificate hanging on the wall stating that Bradley Clevenger was a licensed insurance agent of the great state of Arkansas.

"Bradley, have I ever told you how happy I am you decided to get into the insurance business?"

"No I don't believe you have, but I have no doubt you are. Let's get down to business and get this over with before I tell you what I really think of you."

"You've got the check, don't you Bradley?"

"I've got it and in about twenty-five minutes you will be walking out of here with $600,000 more than you came in with. Come sit down and let's go over the paperwork. I have three forms that I want to read and have you sign."

"Bradley, I don't want to sit here and have you read some legal paperwork to me; can't we just get to the sign-here part of the speech and let me get out of here?"

"Tony, you've played me like a fool since you walked in here with your scheme to get money out of my company. I've broken about every rule I can think of, so why start doing business by the book now?"

"This first form is stating that you have received the check and accepted it as payment in full for the policy covering your business partner, Ricky Alexander."

"Bradley, I don't want to hear anything else. Put the paperwork in front of me, point to where I sign and this day will be over."

"You're the customer – at least for the moment – so let's do it." Bradley aligned the forms one on top of the other, and with a yellow highlighter Bradley simply stated, "Sign here, here, and here."

"Glad to my friend," Tony said, as he started to sign his name. "See, that's not so hard. Now give me my check."

"Almost done; let me get copies of these, and then we will be through." Bradley picked up the papers and started walking down the hallway to the copy room in the back. Instead of turning on the copy machine, Bradley picked up the phone and dialed. Once he heard the phone complete the first ring, he set the phone back on its cradle. He leaned up against the copy machine and looked at the forms he was holding in his hands while in the other room where Tony had been sitting Bradley heard glass breaking followed by the sounds of a struggle.

"That was probably the glass on my insurance license that broke," Bradley thought. The struggle lasted for maybe forty seconds. Then, after a couple of minutes Bradley heard the office door close with a click.

Bradley stayed in the copy room. Footsteps walking down the hall could be heard, and Bradley stared at the doorway in anticipation watching and waiting to see exactly who would appear.

"Good to see you again, Bradley." No-Neck was back acting like a fan again. "Jim Boy is ready to see you now."

Jim Boy stood up when Bradley walked into the room, smiled and extended his hand to Bradley. "Good to see you, Bradley. Now, let's get our paperwork completed." Jim Boy seemed to be in a great mood and truly glad to see Bradley.

"Things had gone as planned," Bradley said. "The first form that Tony signed was the one which stated that he received the check for $600,000. The second form was the check itself. His endorsement meant that it could now be cashed by anyone in possession of the check. The third form was an application that would pay to you the sum of one million dollars in the event of Tony's death. Tony didn't have a clue as to what he was signing.

Jim boy looked over the forms, gave his approval, and handed them back to Bradley. Bradley placed the $600,000 check in an envelope with a deposit slip for Rebecca Alexander's personal account with Bank of America. Bradley intended to go straight to the bank after he mailed the paperwork at the post office. He looked at Jim Boy and told him, "This will go much easier than you can imagine, but I must ask *when will I going to hear something about Tony?*"

"It depends on how quickly they find his body. If no one finds it in a couple of days, a friend of mine will report a body in the Gulpha Gorge Creek. It will appear that the person dove into the creek for a swim and hit his head on a rock. The accident victim ended up with a broken neck and head injuries. It will be ruled an accident, and there will not be an investigation."

"Good. I'll conduct business as usual until I hear something. Then I'll file the claim, and you will get the check for one million in about two weeks."

"Now that's the way I like to do business." Jim Boy was satisfied.

"I may need a favor from you in the future, Jim Boy. Can I count on you?"

"Anytime my friend; I owe you one. Actually I guess it would be more correct to say that I owe you a million."

CHAPTER 26
AN ASSET

"Good afternoon. This is Rose from the Claims department of Premier Insurance Company. Is this Bradley Clevenger, the agent for the Tony LaTour policies?"

"Yes it is. I'm a close friend with the primary beneficiary, Jim Boy. If you will send me the settlement papers, I'll personally deliver them to him myself. I think hand delivery of the money is a valuable service, and it builds trust and loyalty with my clients."

"Bradley, I think you are a great representative of our company and an asset to your community of Hot Springs. Let me go over these final instructions. We have one policy with the insured being Tony LaTour. The amount of the policy is one million dollars, and the primary beneficiary is Jim Boy Baker."

"That is correct," Bradley affirmed.

"The check will be Federal Expressed to your office and will arrive before noon tomorrow. Please sign that the delivery was prompt and all due respect was given."

"Mr. Clevenger, we are sorry for your loss, but glad that you had taken such good care of Mr. LaTour's business partners. Thank you from the Premier Insurance Company, and is there anything else we can do for you?"

Then Bradley answered with a slight grin, "No, thank you," as he turned to look up his travel agent's phone number.

"Hi, this is Alice Naples of Naples' Travel Agency. Where would you like to go?"

"Hi Alice, this is Bradley Clevenger, and I need a one way ticket to Key West."

About the Author

David Tackett was raised in Atkins, Arkansas, a small town he still calls home. After a stint in the Marine Corps and college at the University of Central Arkansas located in Conway, David entered the insurance profession. His insurance career started in Atkins, then to the Kansas City/Lawrence area. He now lives in Hot Springs with his wife Patty. They have three children, Bryan, Chris, and Courtney.

Review Requested:

If you loved this book, would you please provide a review at Amazon.com?

CPSIA information can be obtained
at www.ICGtesting.com
Printed in the USA
FFOW04n1105080517
35309FF